R

"I want to know everything about you, Alain.

"I want to know what makes you the kind of man you are," said Julianna.

"And what kind of man am I?"

"Well-mannered, but aloof. You're really very charming, but beneath that charm is a barrier you won't let anyone cross."

"How do you know that?" he asked.

"I suppose I sense that about you more than I know it."

"Is that what you Americans call intuition?"

"Yes."

"And what else does your intuition tell you?"

"It tells me," she said softly, her next words surprising herself as much as the man with her, "that I'm destined to fall in love with you."

Dear Reader;

This year marks our tenth anniversary and we're having a celebration! To symbolize the timelessness of love, as well as the modern gift of the tenth anniversary, we're presenting readers with a DIAMOND JUBILEE Silhouette Romance title each month, penned by one of your favorite Silhouette Romance authors.

Spend February—the month of lovers—in France with *The Ambassador's Daughter* by Brittany Young. This magical story is sure to capture your heart. Then, in March, visit the American West with Rita Rainville's *Never on Sundae*, a delightful tale sure to put a smile on your lips—and bring ice cream to mind!

Victoria Glenn, Annette Broadrick, Peggy Webb, Dixie Browning, Phyllis Halldorson—to name just a few—have written DIAMOND JUBILEE titles especially for you.

And that's not all! In March we have a very special surprise! Ten years ago, Diana Palmer published her very first romances. Now, some of them are available again in a three-book collection entitled DIANA PALMER DUETS. Each book will have two wonderful stories plus an introduction by the author. Don't miss them!

The DIAMOND JUBILEE celebration, plus special goodies like DIANA PALMER DUETS, is Silhouette Books' way of saying thanks to you, our readers. We've been together for ten years now, and with the support you've given to us, you can look forward to many more years of heartwarming, poignant love stories.

I hope you'll enjoy this book and all of the stories to come. Come home to romance—Silhouette Romance—for always!

Sincerely,

Tara Hughes Gavin
Senior Editor

BRITTANY YOUNG

The Ambassador's Daughter

Published by Silhouette Books New York

America's Publisher of Contemporary Romance

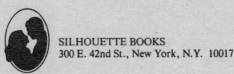

SILHOUETTE BOOKS
300 E. 42nd St., New York, N.Y. 10017

ISBN: 0-373-08700-4

First Silhouette Books printing February 1990

BRITTANY YOUNG

lives and writes in Racine, Wisconsin. She has traveled to most of the countries that serve as the settings for her Romances and finds the research into their languages, customs, history and literature among the most demanding and rewarding aspects of her writing.

A Note From The Author:

Dear Reader:

Romance. What a wonderful word! The images it conjures up are so full of warmth and gentleness, passion and strength. How empty life would be without it, whether in reality or in imagination. Lovers of romance and romance novels are, to me, a very special breed of people who aren't afraid to expose themselves to a range of feelings rarely experienced by others; they're people with heart and soul.

It's been a joy for me during these years with Silhouette Books to put my most romantic imaginings on paper, and a privilege to share those imaginings with readers who feel the same way I do about life and love—and *romance*.

Brittany Young

Chapter One

The ambassador's daughter's sea-green eyes gazed through the window of the limousine as it took her and a woman she'd never met before from the airport away from Paris and headed toward the village of St-Symphorien-le-Château and the home of the Duc de Bournier. It had been a long flight, but Juliana wasn't at all tired. For the first time in more than two years, the entire Sheridan family was going to be together under the same roof. With all seven Sheridan children living in different states and their parents living in Paris, whenever there was a family get-together, someone was always missing. But not this time. It was Claire and Charles Sheridan's fortieth wedding anniversary and the entire family was coming to France to celebrate it with them.

The woman next to her sighed and crossed one shapely leg over the other.

Juliana glanced at her but said nothing. Her attempts at conversation earlier had been, at best, tolerated, but obviously unwelcome. The only things she knew about her were that her name was Noelle, that the two of them had arrived at the airport at approximately the same time and that they were both going to the home of the Duc de Bournier.

The driver watched the women in the rearview mirror whenever traffic would allow. They were a study in contrasts. Juliana's skin was sun kissed and flawless; her lips full and shapely with slightly turned up corners. Her light eyes were surrounded by thick, dark lashes and shone with an appealing dreamy quality. And her hair...

A horn sounded and the driver quickly moved his attention to the road long enough to make a discreet gesture to the offending driver. As soon as everything was clear, his eyes went back to the rearview mirror. Let's see. Where was he? Oh, yes, her hair. How could one describe it? The color was light reddish brown that the sun had gently streaked. A thick mass of curls looped themselves in shining disorder all over her head and reached her shoulders. She was very American and looked as though she belonged out-of-doors in the fresh air.

His gaze moved to the other woman. Her name was Noelle Fouche, his employer's mistress. Her hair was blond and very short, brushed away from her exquisitely pale face to expose high cheekbones and a lovely jawline. She was a beautiful woman, but there was an edge to her beauty. This was a woman who knew exactly what she wanted and how to go about getting it.

The way each woman dressed defined the difference in their personalities even more clearly. Both wore white. Noelle's ultrathin figure was encased in a sleekly sophisticated white suit with a short, pencil-slim skirt. She wore no blouse under the jacket. A heavy gold choker with a horseshoe of diamonds holding it together in the front circled her throat.

Juliana's white skirt was pleated and softly flowing. Her blouse was nautical looking and piped in navy blue, with a blue belt at her slender waist. On the seat next to her was a short-brimmed, flat-topped white hat with a navy-blue band. He could picture her standing on a beach barefoot, staring out to sea. It suited her perfectly.

"Will you be seeing your parents tonight, Mademoiselle Sheridan?" the driver asked in a thick French accent.

Juliana had been deep in her own thoughts. Her eyes met his in the mirror. "Excuse me?"

"I asked if you would be seeing the ambassador and Mrs. Sheridan this evening."

"Oh, no... I'm sorry, I don't know your name."

"Rene."

"Rene. My mother has no idea we're coming. My father is going to spring us all on her at a costume ball as his anniversary gift to her."

"That's nice. Do you have a large family?"

"Six brothers. Three are married. Their wives and children are coming, too."

The driver smiled. "Good. The château could use a few youngsters to liven it up."

"Have any of them arrived yet?"

"One of your brothers and his wife came yesterday. I believe his name is Brian."

Juliana's lovely eyes smiled. Her brothers were all wonderful, but she felt a special closeness to Brian. Despite the ten-year age difference, he'd never minded having her hang around him. She'd been eight when he went to college, but he'd written her letters and called her. When she'd gone to the campus with her parents for a family weekend, Brian had carried her everywhere on his shoulders. To top it off, he'd married a wonderful woman named Sara who, over the years, had evolved into one of Juliana's dearest friends. "Excuse me, Rene, I don't mean to keep quizzing you, but do you know when my other brothers are arriving?"

"I was told to expect them tomorrow."

The Frenchwoman turned her head and eyed Juliana coolly. "Since you're going to be a guest of the Duc's, you should understand that one doesn't speak so informally to servants." There was no effort on Noelle's part to lower her voice so that Rene wouldn't hear.

Juliana was surprised into silence. Her apologetic eyes caught those of the driver in the rearview mirror. Rene winked at her, completely unoffended. A dimple creased Juliana's cheek as she smiled—just a little— then turned her attention to the window. The scenery had grown steadily more rural. "How far away is the

Duc's home, Rene?'' Juliana asked after a few minutes, pointedly ignoring the Frenchwoman's advice.

"The Château de Lumiere is no more than fifteen minutes from here."

"Château de Lumiere," she said softly. "What a pretty name."

"It translates in your language to Castle of Light."

"Is it as lovely as it sounds?''

"Oh, yes, *Mademoiselle*. It is without question one of the most beautiful homes in France. Most of the homes of the old nobility have had to be sold over the years to pay the taxes. The Château de Lumiere is one of the few that is still privately owned—and by the same family who built it over four hundred years ago."

Juliana felt the other woman's eyes on her. She tried to ignore her, but her resolve couldn't overrule her natural instincts. She turned her head to meet the look head-on, more curious than annoyed. It was impossible to read the Frenchwoman's expression and after a moment she gave up trying.

The large car turned down a private road lined on either side with chestnut trees that cast long shadows in the late-afternoon sunlight. "We're on the grounds now," the driver told her.

Juliana returned her gaze to the outside. "How much land is there?"

"There are about one hundred and fifty acres of forest park enclosed by a wall. There used to be much more than that, but over the years some of it has been sold. You'll see the château in just a moment."

Juliana moved forward on her seat and looked through the windshield for her first glimpse of the Duc's home. She didn't have to wait long. As soon as they rounded the next curve, there it was, so beautiful that it literally took her breath away, like a miniature Versailles. In the middle section, three stories of pale stone rose gracefully toward the sky, each story lined with tall, slender windows and capped with a copper cupola that had aged to a pale green. The sections on either side of the middle rose to four stories, each also with a cupola. Six tall chimneys towered over the home. A fountain the size of a pool was visible in the distance with sculpted horses rearing in the center. Juliana glimpsed walkways that stretched in precise patterns among geometrically perfect bushes.

As soon as the car stopped, Juliana opened the car door and stepped onto the crushed gravel driveway to gaze at her surroundings. "Are you sure this is the right place?" she asked in a hushed voïce.

The driver opened the door for the other woman, but his smile was directed at Juliana. "I'm quite sure," he said as he walked to the rear of the car to remove their luggage.

Noelle strode toward the château. "Have my luggage sent to my room," she ordered over her shoulder.

"Yes, *Madame.*"

Juliana waited until she was out of earshot. *"Madame?"* she asked.

"She's divorced," he said quietly. "Please, follow me." He carried her luggage into the château and set it on the cool, tiled floor. Noelle was nowhere to be seen.

Immediately a man dressed in formal attire—the butler, no doubt—approached them through a door that opened off of the foyer.

Juliana smiled at him. "Hello. Do you speak English?"

"Perfectly." There was no return smile.

Juliana sighed inwardly. This wasn't going to be an easy week. "I'm Juliana Sheridan."

"Ah, yes, Miss Sheridan. We've been expecting you. I'll have a maid take you to your room."

"Thank you. Could you tell me where my brother—"

"Juliana!" Brian called out as he walked quickly toward her and pulled her into his arms. "I'm glad you decided to come a day early." He held her away from him, his hands on her shoulders. "You look wonderful. How was your trip?"

"Well, nothing fell off of the plane, if that's what you mean."

"Still afraid to fly, eh?"

Juliana held up her hands. "See these knuckles? Until an hour ago, they were clenched and pure white."

Brian laughed. The corners of his eyes—eyes that were the same sea green as his sister's—crinkled attractively.

"Where's Sara?" she asked, looking over his shoulder and expecting to see her sister-in-law there.

"She's around here somewhere. It's easy to get lost in this place."

"I can imagine. Why are we meeting Mom and Dad here rather than in Paris?"

"Well, as it happens, the ambassador's residence in Paris is undergoing some renovations. Mom and Dad have been staying in a hotel. When the Duc found out what Dad was planning, he offered us the use of all of this," Brian said as he gazed around the foyer. "The Duc is actually the one giving the costume ball on Saturday night."

"Why would he do that for us?"

"He and Dad are friends."

"Have you met him?"

"At dinner last night."

"What's he like?"

Brian ruffled her hair. "I see that glint in your eye."

"What glint?" she asked innocently.

"The glint of a true romantic."

"Oh, Brian, don't start that again."

"Honey, if you're still looking for Prince Charming, believe me when I tell you that this guy isn't him."

"I'm not looking for Prince Charming. I just happen to be selective about the male company I keep. Besides," she asked provocatively, "how can you be so sure he's not P.C.?"

"You'll see for yourself when you meet him. This guy's cold. Ice-cold. How he and Dad ended up friends, I'll never know."

"If Dad likes him, he must have some redeeming qualities."

"Dad likes everyone."

Juliana smiled and a fond warmth filled her eyes. "He does, doesn't he?" Charles Sheridan was a brilliant man. When it came to international politics, there wasn't anything he didn't know, or anyone he couldn't out predict regarding world events. When it came to literature, there wasn't a writer or poet he couldn't quote. But for all of his sharp intelligence, he was a gentle and good man who tended to view mankind without cynicism. He accepted people at face value, until they proved him wrong.

Brian's thoughts echoed his sister's, except that his went a step further. Juliana was a lot like their father. There was a gentleness in her, a vulnerability that made those who loved her very protective of her. She wanted every story to have a happy ending, and real life wasn't like that.

Juliana waved her hand in front of her brother's face. "What on earth are you thinking about?"

Brian smiled. "Nothing important. It's just good to see you. I've missed you."

Juliana hugged him again. "I've missed you, too. I wish you and Sara would move back to Wisconsin."

"That would be a little difficult with both of our jobs in New York. Of course, you could always move there," he suggested.

"And design gardens for concrete lawns? I don't think so."

"I don't think so, either," he said affectionately. "Listen, Juliana Justine, you've had a long day. Go on to your room and get a little rest. I have some things to do but I'll be finished before dinner. And by that time my long-vanished wife should have found her way back."

"What about the Duc? Are we supposed to have dinner with him tonight?"

"I don't know. He went to his office in Paris this morning. Whether he intends coming back for dinner is anyone's guess."

"You mean he actually works?" she asked in feigned amazement. "I thought royalty simply inherited."

"Not this one. He has something to do with international banking."

"So he's gone." Juliana looked thoughtfully at her brother. "That's kind of odd isn't it? What kind of host leaves his guests in the lurch like that?"

"It's not really a host-guest kind of arrangement. He's invited us to use his home as a favor to Dad, but other than that we're pretty much on our own."

Juliana sighed theatrically. "What rotten luck. My first Duc and he's not even here."

Brian grinned at her, then turned to the butler who stood patiently several feet away. "Marcel, is my sister's room ready?"

"Yes, sir. I'll have the maid take her up."

"Thank you." Brian turned back to Juliana. "We'll talk more later."

"Do I have time to do some exploring on my own?"

"Of course. Just don't fall into a black hole the way my wife seems to have done."

"I promise."

Brian kissed her forehead. "See you later."

Marcel returned with a uniformed maid. "Miss Sheridan, this is Yvette. If there's anything you need during the course of your stay, you have but to ask her."

He turned to the maid and gave her some instructions in French and would have left the foyer, but Juliana's voice stopped him. "Marcel?"

He turned, stiffly proper. "Yes?"

"Thank you very much."

Hardier souls than his had been unable to withstand her smile. The butler's eyes softened noticeably as he inclined his head in acknowledgment.

Juliana followed Yvette up a curving marble staircase to the second floor where the hallway was as wide as the foyer, with antique French furniture lining the walls. The doors leading to the bedrooms were white worked with gold and stretched twelve-feet high. Yvette opened a door halfway down the hall. "This is your room, *Mademoiselle* Sheridan. If you need anything, just ask. I'll be up later to unpack for you."

"Thank you, Yvette." Juliana stepped over the threshold and gasped. The canopied bed, which would have overwhelmed an ordinary room, was but a small part of this one. Priceless pieces of Louis XIV furniture were everywhere; a desk with paper and pen at the ready; a small table and chairs; an armoire. A fireplace dominated one wall. On the mantel were Oriental vases at either end and an old, old gold clock that stood about twelve-inches high, glass enclosed so that its inner workings were visible.

Hanging over the mantel was a portrait of a man astride a horse. Juliana moved closer and studied it. In the background was an arch with the year 1654 painted on it. She gazed at the face of the man. He was extraordinarily handsome, with dark hair, a square jaw and dark, brooding eyes that seemed to look directly at her. What had he been thinking when that portrait was painted? Nothing very pleasant, apparently. She looked more closely at his eyes. They were so intense. What a fascinating man he must have been. Who was he? she wondered. What had his life been like?

Juliana backed away from the portrait. It was hard to look away, but she finally forced herself to examine the rest of the room. Heavy draperies that flowed from ceiling to white carpeting were tied away from the French-paned windows. When Juliana looked outside, she saw that they were actually doors that opened onto a balcony. After unhooking the latch, she pushed them open and stepped outside into yet another paradise. Her view stretched across the magnificent lawns and gardens to the woods beyond. Two peacocks, one in full plumage, the other with its tail drifting over the ground like a bridal train, slowly strutted beneath her balcony.

It was all so beautiful that it filled Juliana with a joy that nearly brought her to tears. She wanted to see everything. Looking at her watch, she saw that she had perhaps an hour before the sun set and she was going to make the most of it. Leaving the door to her room wide open behind her, Juliana raced down the marble staircase and out the front door. The limousine was still there. Rene was standing next to the open rear door. As soon as he saw her, he called out and waved her forgotten hat in the air. "You left this on the seat."

Juliana took it from him with a grateful smile and set it on her curls.

Her eyes missing nothing of her surroundings, Juliana walked around the château to the formal gardens. There was a narrow crushed-gravel path she followed through the perfect bushes and around the fountain. Stopping in front of the fountain, she studied the three cast-bronze horses in the middle. Water surged around them making them appear to be rising out of the foam. Their nostrils were flared; each muscle in their strong, lean bodies was defined. It was a powerful work of art.

Crossing the manicured lawn, Juliana walked toward the forest that surrounded the estate and a bark-strewn path that was obviously intended for walkers. Almost immediately she was surrounded by the muffled silence that only comes from forests. The late-afternoon sun shone at an angle through the leaves, dappling the light as it hit the forest floor.

As she stopped walking and reached down to pick a wildflower, she heard the sound of rushing water. Letting her ears be her guide, Juliana found herself near a narrow, shallow stream. Clear water bubbled over softly rounded rocks. She bent next to it and trailed her fingertips through its coolness. In an old childhood habit, her eyes moved over the rocks, stopping when she spotted a particularly pretty one. Standing up straight, she slipped off her shoes, hiked her full skirt above her knees and waded into the stream to retrieve it. Juliana didn't know anything about rocks, but this one looked to her like pink quartz that the water had smoothed over the centuries until it seemed polished.

Climbing out of the water, she sat on the grassy bank, her skirt spread out around her, and gently rubbed the stone between her fingers. As a child she had picked up rocks similar to this along the shores of Lake Michigan. She'd carried them around the way the Greeks carried worry beads, examining every irregularity with her fingertips until the rock was memorized. When she wanted to think, or to dream, she would pull one out of her pocket and absently run her fingertips over it while her thoughts took wing.

They did that now as she recreated in her mind the portrait over the fireplace. If she closed her eyes, she could remember the man exactly. Those eyes.

A small frown creased her forehead. She hadn't heard any sound, but she was suddenly aware that she wasn't alone. Juliana slowly opened her eyes and turned her head. Her mouth parted softly in wonder. A man sat astride a horse on an incline less than ten yards away. He was wearing tan riding pants and black riding boots and a white shirt, open at his throat with the sleeves rolled partially up his tanned and powerful forearms. His hair was dark, and even in the fading light, she could make out the carved features of his handsome face.

Juliana slowly rose. Her eyes met his dark, intense ones and locked. Neither of them said anything. Juliana's heart pounded beneath her breast. He was her portrait come to life and the power he held over her was hypnotic. She couldn't speak; she couldn't move. She could only stare at him.

His eyes left hers to move over her face. His jaw clenched. Still in silence, he wheeled his great horse around and rode away from her.

The minute his eyes left hers, Juliana came back to life. Hiking up her skirt, her hand still clutching the rock, she raced barefoot after him, up the incline and across the path. Frantically she looked in the direction in which he'd ridden off, but he was already gone. She ran farther, stopping here and there and looking in all directions. Her hat flew off her head, but she didn't notice. Where was he? She felt something close to panic. *What if she never saw him again?*

The minutes ticked by as though in slow motion. She searched until it was almost too dark to see, then reluctantly gave up and made her way back to the stream for her shoes. Sinking onto the grass, she slipped on her shoes, a faraway look in her eyes. What if the man hadn't really been there at all? What if she'd simply imagined the man in the portrait had come to life?

Wrapping her arms around her legs, she hugged her knees to her chest and rested her chin on them. She could hear the sounds of the night creatures of the forest as they woke. Insects chattered. Leaves rustled in the light breeze. The noise of the stream was muffled by the darkness.

Juliana wasn't at all frightened. If anything, the darkness was comforting. Tranquil.

"Who are you?" she asked the night. "Where did you come from and where did you go?"

She moved her fingertips over her rock. "And will I ever see you again?"

Chapter Two

Juliana showered and changed from her traveling clothes into a full-skirted dress the same green color as her eyes. Eyeing herself in the mirror, she wrinkled her nose. Her hair. No matter how she tried to style it, it refused to be tamed.

Giving up on it, she sprayed herself lightly with her favorite cologne, then crossed the room to the fireplace to gaze at the portrait. It had been nearly an hour since her walk in the forest. Had she really seen him out there or had her imagination been playing tricks on her?

Standing on a footstool in front of the fireplace, Juliana reached out to trace the line of his jaw with her fingertips, and rested them on his carved mouth. "Was it you in the forest?" she whispered. "Why did you run away from me? If it was you, give me a sign of some kind.''

There was a knock.

Juliana's eyes widened for a moment, then she shook her head and smiled at herself. ''Nah.'' Climbing down from the stool, she opened the door.

''Juliana!'' her sister-in-law cried happily as she wrapped her warmly in her arms. ''I'm so glad you're here.''

Juliana hugged her tightly, then held her at arm's length and looked at her. Sara was a very pretty woman, with soft brown hair and bright blue eyes. ''Oh, Sara, you look wonderful. Your hair looks good when it's longer.''

''I like it, too, but I wish it was less trouble to take care of. I'm sorry I wasn't around when you got here.''

''Brian said you were exploring.''

''Boy, was I ever. And what a house to explore! It goes on forever.''

''Did you find anything interesting?''

''I think an easier question to answer would be if I found anything that *isn't* interesting. There's so much history here, it's remarkable. Did you know that Marie Antoinette used to come here to visit a member of the de Bournier family? Brian and I have the room she used to sleep in.''

''Marie Antoinette? I can't even conceive...'' She shook her head. ''Can you imagine living in a place like this?''

''I'd love it. Wouldn't you?''

"I don't know. I think I'd spend so much time lost in my imagination that I'd forget about the real world."

"Since when do you mind forgetting about the real world?"

Juliana narrowed an eye at her sister-in-law. "Don't you start on me now. I have to put up with enough of that from Brian."

"He is rather down-to-earth, isn't he?"

"That's the understatement of the decade."

"All right. I hereby promise not to pull a Brian on you."

"Thank you. Have you been outside at all?"

"Not yet."

"I was out exploring the forest for a little while this evening. You really have to make a point of getting out. The grounds are the most beautiful I've ever seen."

"This, from a woman who designs other people's gardens. I'm impressed."

"So was I." Juliana turned her head and looked at the portrait. "While I was out," she said idly, turning her attention back to Sara, "I saw a man riding a big black horse. Would you have any idea who that might have been?"

"Well, the Duc is the only one who lives here but I think he's gone off on business somewhere."

"That's what Brian said."

"Maybe one of the stable hands."

"No," Juliana said quietly, "this was no stable hand."

"If it's important, I'm sure you could ask one of the servants. They should know."

"Perhaps I will."

Sara looked at her sister-in-law curiously. "Is everything all right?"

"Of course. Why?"

"I don't know exactly. You seem a little... distracted."

Juliana gave her a reassuring smile. "I think this place makes everyone seem distracted."

Sara shook her head. "No, it isn't that. Did the man on the horse do or say anything to upset you?"

"Upset me? No, not at all. The only reason I even brought it up was that I was curious about him. He sort of appeared out of nowhere and disappeared the same way."

Sara wasn't convinced, but she dropped it. She'd known and loved Juliana for more than ten years, and in that time she'd learned never to press too hard. If something was on her mind, Juliana would tell her when she was ready. She looped her arm through Juliana's and squeezed it close to her side. "Come on, let's go downstairs together. Brian's already there." She shook her head. "Poor man. He spends half his life waiting for me."

Juliana glanced back at the portrait one last time before walking away. "He must not mind too much."

"To be honest, I think he does, but he's too polite to say so, even to me."

With their arms still joined, they went down the stairs to a room whose tall double doors opened off the foyer.

Brian was already there, sitting on a couch deep in thought, a drink in his hand. He smiled and rose as soon as they entered. "I see you found each other."

Sara went up on her toes and kissed his cheek. "More importantly, we found you; not an easy task in this house."

A servant entered the room and bowed politely. "May I get you something to drink?"

Sara thought for a moment. "White wine, please."

He turned to Juliana.

"Just mineral water for me, thank you."

With another inclination of his head, he left the room.

Sara sighed as she sank onto the couch. "I could get used to this." She touched Brian's arm as he sat next to her. "Remind me when we get back to New York that I want to hire a servant. Maybe several of them."

Brian smiled and shook his head. "You definitely married the wrong guy."

Sara smiled back at him, and the love they felt for each other was evident in their eyes.

Juliana watched them wistfully. She was twenty-five years old and she'd never in her life felt that way about anyone. Nor was she willing to settle for anything less.

Instead of sitting, Juliana wandered around the room. Like those portions of the house that she'd seen so far, it was a formal room, designed more for elegance than comfort. Its sheer size was daunting. Floor-to-ceiling French-paned doors lined one wall entirely and several of them were open to let in the cool night air. Wonderful music floated softly around the room.

As soon as the servant had returned with her drink, Juliana walked to one of those doors and stood looking outside. The fountain she'd admired earlier was lit and the spray of water coming from it sparkled like diamonds against the black velvet of the sky.

"It's lovely, isn't it?" Sara asked.

Juliana nodded without turning around. "Like everything about this place, it's like something out of a fantasy."

"But it's not a fantasy, Miss Sheridan. It's very real. You would do well to remember that."

She turned to find Noelle Fouche standing in the doorway, stunning and sleek in black. The Frenchwoman spoke to someone out of sight, then stepped farther into the room, but Juliana had no idea what the woman did after that. Her eyes were riveted on the man who'd entered behind Noelle. He was the man in her portrait; the man by the stream. Juliana's heart pounded. She could literally feel her blood moving through her veins. His dark eyes—the same as the eyes in the portrait—locked with hers. Juliana vaguely heard him introduce himself. His name was Alain, Duc de Bournier. The other voices in the room had faded so much into the background of her mind that she couldn't understand a single word that was said to her.

The man walked toward her, his eyes never leaving hers. The closer he came, the harder her heart pounded until she felt breathless. Standing directly in front of her, he took her hand in his. Someone must have introduced them because he said her name in a deep, rich voice with just a hint of an accent.

"Are you cold, Miss Sheridan?" he asked.

She tried with near desperation to concentrate on what he was saying. "Excuse me?"

His eyes moved over her suddenly pale face. "You're trembling. I asked if you were cold."

She couldn't think of a single plausible reason for trembling other than cold. "A little, I guess."

He released her hand and moved past her to close the doors, then spoke to the servant who'd followed him into the room.

Sara walked over to Juliana. "Are you all right?" she whispered in concern. "You look as though you've seen a ghost."

"No, I'm fine, really." She tried to sound reassuring, but the quaver in her voice seemed to worry her sister-in-law all the more.

Sara took Juliana by the hand and walked her to the couch, placing her between Brian and herself. Then she took the mineral water away from Juliana and put her own glass of wine in her hand. "Drink it," she said softly. "It can only help."

Juliana took a delicate sip.

"Don't sip it, girl," she hissed. "Drink it."

Juliana downed it in two gulps.

Sara took the glass and looked around Juliana to her husband. "Where's a good stiff cognac when you really need one?"

"I'm fine, Sara. Please stop fussing over me." And she was. After the initial shock of seeing the portrait come to life, she'd pulled herself together. She watched the Duc as he spoke quietly to the servant. He'd

changed into a dark, double-breasted suit, striped shirt
and tie. The jacket was unbuttoned and he stood with
one hand in his trousers pocket. Noelle was beside him.
They were a stunning-looking couple.

When the servant had gone, the Duc and Noelle sat
on the couch across from Juliana, Sara and Brian.
Again, his eyes went to Juliana's. "Are you warmer
now, Miss Sheridan?"

"Yes, thank you. And please call me Juliana."

"Juliana." He softened the first letter of her name so
that it sounded like a caress. "And you must call me
Alain."

She could have looked at him forever. Her eyes
moved over his face feature by feature, resting for a
moment on his carved mouth before moving back to his
eyes. "Was it you I saw riding in the forest earlier this
evening?" she asked quietly, oblivious to the others in
the room.

"I was there."

"Did you see me?"

"Yes."

"Why didn't you speak?"

"You rose out of the mist by the stream," he said
softly. "Until I walked into this room and saw you, I
thought you were but a figment of my imagination."

There was a sudden commotion in the doorway and
another man entered. He was tall and very slender with
an openly handsome face. After speaking to the servant in French, he walked toward the others in the
room, eyeing the trio on the couch in general and Juliana in particular. "You must be the Americans my

cousin has been expecting.'' He extended his hand to Brian, who along with Alain had risen, and then to Sara and Juliana. He held Juliana's hand in his for a lot longer than was necessary, until she politely extricated herself.

The Duc looked something less than pleased. ''This is my cousin, Jacques Perney,'' he introduced. ''I assume that you'll be staying for dinner, Jacques?''

''Oh, yes. Dinner is why I came in the first place. I was certain that your failure to invite me was an oversight on your part, Alain.'' He squeezed himself between Juliana and Sara, smiling at Juliana the entire time. ''You must let me show you Paris while you're here.''

''I appreciate the offer, but I don't think I'll be doing very much sight-seeing during the short time I'm in France.''

''You could always extend that time.''

It was impossible not to like Jacques. He was pure impudence, but pulled it off charmingly. He reminded her of her business partner in Wisconsin. Benjamin had that same kind of appeal. Juliana smiled at him.

Jacques smiled back. ''I think,'' he said to the Duc without once removing his eyes from Juliana, ''that I'm going to be spending quite a bit of time here for the next week or so.''

A servant walked in at that moment and whispered something to Alain. The Duc nodded, then rose and looked at Brian. ''I'm sorry, but something has come up. I won't be able to have dinner with you as I had hoped. There are some business matters I must attend to in Paris.''

Brian rose also and extended his hand. "Please don't apologize. It's more than enough that you're making your home so open to us.''

The Duc turned to Juliana. His eyes moved slowly over her face. "Do you ride?''

"Oh, yes," she said with a smile. "Our parents have a home in the country. We all grew up with horses.''

"Of course some of us spent more time on the ground than on the horse," Brian interjected. "Do you ride, Noelle?''

"No." She was no more interested in talking now than she had been in the car. It was as though just sitting there with them was a form of penance.

"I hope you will all feel free to ride any of my horses whenever you wish," Alain said, his eyes on Juliana.

"That's very kind of you," she replied softly.

His dark eyes grew darker. "I'm a good host. It doesn't necessarily follow that I'm a kind man." He looked at Brian and Sara and bowed slightly. "I'll see you all tomorrow. I hope you have a pleasant evening." Then he turned to Noelle. "Get your things. I'm taking you back to Paris with me.''

She looked at him in surprise and spoke rapidly in French.

He said one word, also in French.

Noelle was instantly silent, but certainly not pleased. Rising abruptly, she left the room. Alain followed her out.

"Well, that's my cousin for you.''

Juliana turned to Jacques. "What do you mean?"

"His manners are impeccable, but he has all the personal charm and warmth of a stingray."

"I like him."

He looked at Juliana in surprise. "You're kidding."

"She likes everyone," Sara said.

"For heaven's sake, you make me sound like a puppy. That's not true. I just think he's the kind of person who doesn't show others what he's feeling."

"Oh, no," Jacques said as he dramatically put his hand over his heart. "Don't tell me you're one of those."

"One of those what?"

"A romantic."

"You know," Juliana said impatiently, "you're the fourth person who's labeled me a romantic in the past month. I've tried to deny it, but I'm not going to any longer. Yes, I'm a romantic, and I'm proud of it."

Jacques clicked his tongue.

"Now what?"

"Be careful."

"Be careful? Why?"

"Life has a way of disillusioning those who dare to be of a romantic nature."

"I'm doing just fine so far."

"So far. But you've only been in France for a day." His tone was ominous, but his eyes were twinkling.

Juliana laughed. "I'm glad you came for dinner."

"So am I. And you can bet that I'll be back for breakfast."

A servant walked in at that moment to tell them that dinner was served. All four of them rose to follow him from the room, but Brian caught Juliana's arm to hold her back for just a moment. "Sara, you go on with Jacques. We'll be there in a minute."

Juliana looked at her brother curiously. "What's wrong, Brian? You look so serious."

"I am. Don't you let yourself fall for him. He's nothing like the kind of man who will make you happy."

"Jacques? He's fun, but he's certainly not anyone I'd fall in love with. Besides, we just met."

"I'm not talking about Jacques. He's harmless enough. I'm talking about the Duc."

Juliana was so taken aback that she couldn't think of anything intelligent to say.

"I saw the way you looked at him when he walked into the room. I've known you all of your life and I've never seen you look at anyone like that before."

"Brian . . ."

He lifted his hand. "Hear me out, please. The Duc isn't like you and me. Juliana, you're a lovely woman, inside and out. He may well be attracted to you, but you can bet he'll move on before too long, and he'll certainly never consider a future with you. You'd be deluding yourself to think otherwise."

"Are you finished now?"

He nodded.

Juliana shook her head. "Brian, you're my brother and I love you."

"I hear a but in there somewhere."

"What I choose to do with my life is no one's business but mine. I appreciate your concern, but it isn't necessary. I'm a big girl and I can take care of myself. I've been doing just that for a very long time."

"You may be a big girl, as you put it, but you're still my little sister."

"Please, let's not argue about it."

"All right. I just wanted to say my piece and I've done that."

"Indeed you have." Juliana reached up and kissed his cheek. "You're the best brother a girl could have."

"This is true."

"Not to mention modest."

Sara poked her head around the corner. "Are you two going to stand here talking all night? I'm hungry."

"Sorry." Brian held out both of his arms. Juliana took one, Sara the other, and the three of them walked to the dining room to join Jacques.

Once again, Juliana found herself overwhelmed by the sheer size of a room. It was nothing short of a banquet hall that could easily handle a hundred people. Chandeliers lined the length of the ceiling. The table went on and on and on. The four places that were formally set at one end were dwarfed. A servant stood behind each chair.

"Pretty impressive, eh?" Sara said out of the corner of her mouth as they walked the length of the table to their seats.

Juliana didn't say anything until after they were seated, then she turned to Jacques who was next to her. "When the Duc eats alone, does he eat in here?"

"Yes, he does."

She found that unutterably sad.

But despite that and the formal setting, the four of them managed to have a wonderful time. Brian, Sara and Juliana caught up on one another's news and enjoyed Jacques's running commentary, while at the same time experiencing a culinary masterpiece that began with a rich vegetable soup and *corne au jambon*. Then there was filet mignon, potato souffleé and asparagus with béchamel sauce. Juliana passed on the warm Brie, but when the éclair *au chocolat* found its way in front of her, she couldn't resist. There had been a different wine for every course, which Juliana left untouched except for a polite sip of each. And finally, coffee with cognac.

Juliana leaned back in her seat and sighed. "It's going to take twenty-four straight hours of running to work off these calories. And I don't regret a bite."

"That's what I like. A woman who can eat without remorse," her brother said. "Personally I'm ready to fall asleep."

"Wonderful," Sara said dryly. "We're in a romantic castle in France, we've just shared an incredible meal and all you want to do is sleep."

Brian wiggled his eyebrows. "Not necessarily alone."

"Oh, well, why didn't you say so in the first place. You're forgiven."

As Juliana started to rise, the man behind her pulled out her chair. "I think this is the point where the sister makes a graceful exit."

"As well as the unrelated bystander," said Jacques, rising as well. "What are you going to do with the rest of your evening, Juliana?"

"I hope you don't mind, Jacques, but I think I'll just go to my room. It's been a long day."

"Then I'll take my leave. Come and walk me to the door."

"All right." She walked around the table and kissed Brian and Sara. "I'll see you both in the morning."

"Not me," Brian said as he stretched his arms high over his head. "I have to go into Paris in the morning to make a few last-minute plans for the party on Saturday."

"Anything I can help with?" she offered.

"No. It's nothing major. I'll be back in the afternoon—certainly before the rest of the family gets here."

"Good night, then."

Jacques held out his arm. "Come on, Juliana."

She placed her hand on his arm and the two of them walked down the long hallway to the foyer. He opened the door and turned to look at Juliana. "I really would like to have the chance to spend some time with you while you're here."

"As I said earlier, that will be difficult."

"I know." He smiled and his eyes crinkled at the corners. "I like you."

She smiled back. "I like you, too."

"See you tomorrow."

Juliana watched until he'd driven away, then closed the door and started up the stairs. She was about halfway up when she stopped. What was she doing? She didn't really want to go to her room. She wanted to be outside. Turning around, she went back to the room where they'd had cocktails. The doors had been opened again. The music still played softly. She took off her shoes and dangled them from one hand as she stepped outside. Taking a deep breath, she exhaled on a long sigh. It was probably midnight, perhaps later, but she wasn't at all tired. She was just glad to be alone with her thoughts and the music.

Swaying gently back and forth, she began dancing with an imaginary partner, turning and turning her way down the path toward the fountain, unaware of the man watching her until she bumped into him. Alain caught her in his arms and steadied her.

Juliana looked up at him in surprise and a little embarrassment. "I'm sorry. I didn't know you were there."

"Obviously. Do you often dance alone?"

"No comment." Juliana stepped back and Alain's arms fell to his sides. "How long have you been back?"

"Not long."

"You missed a wonderful dinner."

"I ate in Paris."

"Of course." She looked around. "Where's Noelle?"

"She stayed in Paris."

Juliana turned to gaze at the subtly lit fountain, tinglingly aware of the man beside her.

"You're up late for someone who's spent the day traveling."

"I'm only going to be here for a week. I don't want to waste my time on sleep."

"Have you ever been to France before?"

"When I was a teenager. I only got to see Paris, though."

"Only Paris?"

"I didn't mean that the way it sounded," she said with a smile. "I loved Paris, but I'm much more of a country person than a city person." She gazed at the fountain.

The Frenchman gazed at her.

"Does anyone live here besides you?"

"Only servants."

"It must get lonely at times."

"At times."

"I take it your parents are dead?"

"They both died in an accident when I was ten."

Juliana turned her head to look at him and touched his arm in sympathy. "That's awful. I'm so sorry."

He shrugged. "I didn't know them very well anyway. I can't honestly say that their deaths made a big difference in my life."

Juliana was genuinely shocked. "How can it not have made a big difference?"

Alain looked at Juliana and smiled. "Don't sound so outraged. My parents weren't like yours. I was raised entirely by nannies and governesses. When my parents were here, I was brought to my mother for ten minutes a day."

Juliana's lovely eyes filled with a sadness that she couldn't disguise.

Alain's mouth curved. "Don't look at me like that. I grew up just fine without them."

"But you were alone."

"I like being alone. I always have."

"Is that why you haven't married?"

"I haven't married because I haven't met a woman I felt I could live with."

"What about love?"

"What about it?"

"Isn't that important to you?"

"No." He looked down at her. "You seem shocked."

"I am. Have you ever been in love?"

"I thought I was once. I was seven. She was twenty-four. Needless to say, it didn't work out."

Juliana's laughter lightly rippled the air. "Was she a governess?"

"Yes, but unfortunately not a very good one. She only lasted four weeks. It very nearly broke my heart when my father fired her."

Juliana's smile faded into a sigh as she gazed into the fountain.

Alain studied her profile. "I thought to make you laugh and I did, but now you seem sad again."

"I just know how important my family has always been to me," she said quietly. "I can't imagine my life without them."

"And so you pity me."

"I guess in that respect, yes."

A corner of his mouth lifted. "This is new to me. With most of the people I meet, pity is just about the last emotion I would imagine they have."

"I'm not most people."

"I'm beginning to understand that."

Juliana turned her head and looked into his eyes. Her heart moved into her throat.

Alain's eyes moved over her face feature by feature. "Are you this interested in everyone you meet?"

"No. But with you, it's somehow different. I want to know everything about you. I want to know what makes you the kind of man you are."

"And what kind of man am I?"

"Well mannered, but aloof. You're really very charming, but beneath that charm is a barrier you won't let anyone cross."

"How do you know that?"

"I suppose I sense that about you more than I know it."

"Is that what you Americans call intuition?"

"Yes."

"And what else does your intuition tell you?"

"It tells me," she said softly, her next words surprising herself as much as the man with her, "that I'm destined to fall in love with you."

Alain looked at her in silence for a long time before placing his index finger under her chin and raising her eyes to his. He shook his head. "You would be making a big mistake to allow that to happen."

"So I've heard."

"Why do you think this?"

"When I first went to my room, I saw a portrait of a man. I was very drawn to it without understanding why. Then I saw you on the horse, and again I felt something I couldn't explain." She shook her head. "I'm not making sense. You see, it's as though I've known all my life what the man who is to be my destiny looked like. It wasn't anything conscious. I was just comfortable with his image without even realizing the image was there. You are him.''

Alain rubbed the soft skin of her cheek with his thumb. ''What a strange young woman you are.''

Juliana's lips parted as she looked into his eyes. ''You haven't known me long enough to judge me strange.''

''And you haven't known me long enough to judge me your destiny,'' he said quietly.

''Then it would appear that we both have a lot to learn about each other.''

''Juliana, you're a beautiful woman, and I'm as susceptible as the next man. But if anything were to happen between us, it would be only for that moment and nothing more.''

''How do you know?''

''Because that's all I would allow.''

''All right. I'll consider myself warned.''

His eyes moved over her face. ''You don't believe me, do you?''

''I think you're quite sincere.''

''But you don't think it relates to you?''

''I don't know,'' she said quietly. ''But as I said to someone just this evening, I'm a big girl.''

Alain looked at her for a moment longer, then dropped his hand to his side and turned toward the fountain. ''Go inside, Juliana. It's late and you should be sleeping.''

She gazed at his profile. In this light, with the shadows playing across his face, he seemed almost haunted.

There was no other word she could think of to describe
it. "Good night, Alain."

He didn't look at her. "Good night."

When she had gone, he turned toward the house and
watched until the light came on in her room. He saw her
silhouette as she passed in front of the window.

"Oh, woman," he said softly in French, "where did
you come from? Surely nowhere as mundane as Wisconsin. You're like some innocent sent to earth by the
gods to taunt me."

Alain dragged his fingers through his thick hair and
started walking away from the house. Away from her.

Juliana slipped into her nightgown and turned out the
light. Instead of going to bed, though, she went outside on the balcony. She could see Alain standing by the
fountain. She watched as he walked away, his hands in
his pockets.

She couldn't believe what she'd said to him. But there
wasn't a word of it that she would have taken back even
if she could have. What she'd said had come from her
heart. Even she wasn't aware of it until the words were
between them.

She crossed her arms over her breasts and hugged
herself. She was frightened and hopeful all at the same
time.

And confused.

How was it possible to know a man for such a short
time, and yet be so sure that he was the one?

How was it possible to know, as she did, within the very core of her being, that she loved him the way she could never love another man?

All of this she knew without a word from him. Without a kiss. Without a touch.

All of this she knew.

Chapter Three

Juliana woke to another beautiful day. She lay in bed, nestled under the sheets, and studied the elaborate moldings that circled the ceiling, wondering about others who'd lain exactly where she was now, perhaps hundreds of years ago, looking at the same moldings and thinking about—what?

She tried to rein in her thoughts, but whenever she did, Alain's darkly handsome face floated before her. Her gaze moved to the portrait over the fireplace and remained there for several minutes.

Closing her eyes, Juliana rested her hand on her stomach. She could literally feel it flutter. She took a deep calming breath and slowly exhaled. Whatever was going to happen was going to happen. All she could do was be herself and take things as they came.

With a joyful shake of her head, Juliana got up and took a quick shower. After searching through the drawers the maid had arranged for her the night before, she pulled out a pair of khaki shorts with cuffs and a white, short-sleeved T-shirt. Sitting on the edge of the bed, she laced up her white sneakers and headed out of her room. She met Sara coming up the stairs as she was going down. "Hi! What are you doing up so early?"

"Seeing Brian off."

"Oh, that's right. He's going to Paris. Why didn't you go with him?"

"I'm a little tired today. I want to just stay here and rest. What about you? What are you going to do?"

"Look around. Perhaps find a book and do some quiet reading."

"That's a good idea. Once the rest of the family gets here this afternoon, the time for doing anything 'quiet' will be a thing of memory."

"I know," Juliana said with a smile. "I'm looking forward to the chaos. Do you think Alain would mind if I borrowed a book from his library?"

"He wouldn't," said a voice from the top of the stairs.

Juliana looked up to find Alain standing there. He had on casual, loose fitting charcoal-colored trousers. The collar of his white shirt showed above the crew neck of his gray sweater. "Good morning," she said quietly.

"Good morning, Juliana," he said as he drew level with her. "Sara." He inclined his head toward the other woman.

Sara looked curiously from one to the other of them. "Well," she said awkwardly after a moment, "I think I'll head back to my room."

"I'll talk to you later," Juliana called after her as Sara disappeared up the stairs. Taking a deep breath, she turned to Alain. "I brought a book with me to read on the plane but I've finished it already."

"Don't worry about it. I have books to spare. Come. I'll take you to the library."

They started down the stairs. "Have you had breakfast?" he asked.

"No. I don't eat in the morning."

Alain looked at her sideways. "You should. You're too slender."

Juliana's sea-green eyes sparkled.

"What's so funny?"

"I was feeling guilty about the enormous dinner I ate last night. You just saved me a lot of running time."

Alain's eyes moved to her tousled hair.

She self-consciously tugged on a curl and released it to return to its natural curve. "There's not a thing I can do with it. It's been this way since I was born."

His dark eyes softened. "I like your hair exactly the way it is."

It was a small enough compliment, but it warmed Juliana immeasurably.

As they talked, they walked down one hallway after another, turning corners until Juliana had no idea where she was. They finally came to an open door. "Here," Alain said as he stood aside to let Juliana enter first.

"You realize, of course, that I'm going to need a map to find my way back."

"It's not as complicated as you think."

Juliana stepped into the room and gasped. It was worthy of a museum. First editions in every language imaginable lined the shelves in glass-enclosed cases. Oil paintings of portraits and landscapes filled any vacant wall space. The furniture was elegant and uncomfortable looking. There were several reading tables. The room itself was so large that she had to speak louder to make herself heard by Alain at the other end. "I don't suppose you have anything as mundane as, say, an Agatha Christie novel?"

"I'm afraid not."

She looked inside the cases but didn't touch anything. She was afraid to. Everything was so valuable.

"Here's what I was looking for." Alain lifted a book from one of the shelves and crossed the room to her.

Juliana took it from him and read the title aloud. *"The Life And Work Of George Gordon, Lord Byron."* She looked at him curiously. "Why would you pick this for me?"

"You just strike me as someone who would be an admirer of the man and his poetry. And, as you can see," he said as he tapped the leather binding, "it's in English."

"Well, his personal life left something to be desired, but you're right about his poetry. My father introduced me to it when I was about thirteen and I've loved it ever since." She looked up at him. "Thank you."

He inclined his dark head, his eyes on hers.

"Do you ever read Byron?"

"I have, but I'm not a fan. He's a little too romantic for my tastes."

"Oh."

"Oh? You sound disappointed."

"It's just that you dislike him for the very reason that I enjoy him."

"Surely that doesn't surprise you. We're obviously two very different people."

"In some ways, but there's nothing wrong with that."

"No. Not as long as we remember it."

She looked into his eyes. "You're determined to keep me at arm's length, aren't you?"

"It's for your own good."

Juliana shook her head. "No. You're looking out for yourself, not for me."

"I'm doing what?"

"You heard me."

"Yes, I heard you, but I'm not quite sure that I know what you mean."

Juliana just smiled at him.

Alain looked at her with narrowed eyes. "Juliana Sheridan, I don't know you well at all, but even so, there are times when I find you infuriating."

Her smile grew. "Good. There's nothing worse than complacency. Now I'm going to find a nice, quiet place to read. I'll return the book when I'm finished."

"There you are!" said Jacques from the doorway. "I've been looking all over for you, Juliana." He smiled at Alain. "Hello, cousin. I hope you don't mind, but I have every intention of appropriating your guest for as long as she'll allow me."

"Juliana's time is her own," Alain said, suddenly formal. He looked at Juliana, bowed stiffly and left.

"I see he's his usual cheerful self," Jacques said when he'd gone.

"Actually he was just fine until you came."

"I should have guessed that. We've never been what you'd call close."

"So I gathered. Why not?"

"We're very different people with nothing at all in common."

"Where have I heard that before?"

"Excuse me?"

Juliana smiled and shook her head. "Nothing. Are your parents living?"

"Yes."

"Is it your mother or your father who's related to Alain?"

"My mother, twice removed. I'm afraid I'm from the untitled side of the family."

Juliana looked at him in surprise. "You sound almost bitter, Jacques."

"I guess I am a little." He looked around the room. "It's all an accident of birth. This could all have been mine."

"Would you be happier if it were?"

"I don't know. I'd definitely be richer," he conceded after a moment's thought.

"That certainly put things in perspective," she said with a smile.

"I admit it. I like money as much as the next man. Women like money, too. And women like men who have money. Take Noelle for instance. She won't even look at me now, but if Alain and I were to change places financially, I'd be the one she'd want."

"I think you're shortchanging Alain. He's a very attractive man with or without his money."

"Only an American," Jacques said with amusement. He took the book from her hands and read the binding. "And one who reads Byron at that. You probably find my cousin mysterious."

"A little."

"And a challenge."

"Very much."

"And you think that he'd be different with you than he is with anyone else."

Juliana nodded.

"You're deluding yourself."

"That does seem to be the popular opinion."

"Men don't change. They are the way they are."

"Yet another popular opinion."

Jacques laughed. "Come on, Juliana Sheridan. Let's go find a nice spot and follow the travails of Childe Harold, though personally my favorite poem of his is, uh, let me see if I can remember how it goes." He thought for a moment and then began:

"She was a Phantom of delight
When first she gleamed upon my sight;
A lovely Apparition, sent
To be a moment's ornament;

Her eyes as stars of Twilight fair;
Like Twilight's, too, her dusky hair;
But all things else about her drawn
From May-time and the cheerful Dawn;
A dancing Shape, an Image gay,
To haunt, to startle, and way-lay."

He looked at her and smiled. "Not bad, eh?"

"It's wonderful—except that it's not Byron."

"It's not?"

"No. Wordsworth."

"You're sure?"

"Positive."

"How disappointing, not to mention humiliating." He clicked his tongue. "Perhaps Byron doesn't have as much going for him as I thought."

"Does that mean you've changed your mind about reading him with me?"

Jacques grinned at her. "Not a chance. Though I'd prefer that you do the reading so I can do the listening."

"You'd be content doing that?"

"Oh, pretty woman, I'd be content to spend the morning doing nothing but looking at you."

"Thank you," she said with a smile. "That's a charming thing to say."

"I know."

Her smile grew wider.

"Not necessarily true, but charming nonetheless." Jacques took her arm. "I know the perfect tree to lean against while we read."

"I'm sure you do."

Instead of walking all through the house, he took her to a door that was close by, leading to a garden she hadn't seen yet. There was a wonderful ancient thick-trunked tree in the middle of it and that's where they went. Juliana raised her face to the sky as they sat on the grass. "This is perfect."

"Yet another appalling American trait."

"What's that?" She opened her eyes a slit and glanced over at him.

"This ridiculous worship of the sun."

"It's warm and cheerful."

"Exactly my point."

"If it helps any, I'm equally fond of cloudy days," she told him.

"You're just saying that to cheer me up."

"You're a hard man to please."

"How much of an effort are you willing to make?" he asked with a mischievous smile behind his eyes.

"You have a one-track mind, Jacques. Sit back and I'll read to you."

"That's it? You'll read to me?"

"That's it."

Jacques sighed and leaned back against the tree. "Well, it better be good."

Juliana lay on her stomach with the book propped in front of her. She carefully paged through it until she found the passages she was looking for, and then in her pleasant voice, began to read, unaware of the dark eyes watching from the house.

The air around them was still except for the restful singing of the birds. Juliana lost track of time.

"All Heaven and Earth are still—though not in sleep,
But breathless, as we grow when feeling most;
And silent, as we stand in thoughts too deep: —
All Heaven and Earth are still: From the high host
Of stars, to the lull'd lake and mountain coast,
All is concentered in a life intense,
Where not a beam, nor air, nor leaf is lost,
But hath a part of Being, and a sense
Of that which is of all Creator and defence."

Juliana closed the book and sighed a dreamy sigh. "Isn't that wonderful?"

There was no answer.

"Jacques?"

There was still no answer.

She looked up to find him sound asleep, still leaning against the trunk of the tree.

She laughed softly. "Another inspirational reading taken to heart. Jacques? Jacques? I've finished reading. It's safe to wake up now."

He opened one eye. "Are you sure?"

"Quite."

"Ah." He straightened his back. "What shall we do now?"

"We could go for a walk."

"Well you're just full of all kinds of avant-garde suggestions, aren't you?"

"Do you have a better idea?"

He looked her up and down. "Several, but something tells me you'd say 'no.'"

"Something tells me I would, too."

Jacques sighed. "That's really too bad. You and I together." He kissed his fingertips. "Incredible."

"Incredible is the word all right." Juliana looked at her watch and sat up abruptly. "Oh, I had no idea it was so late."

"Indeed, time flies when you're reading Byron," Jacques said dryly.

Juliana lightly slapped his arm. She was remarkably comfortable with him. "I have some things to do before the rest of my family gets here."

"Will I see you later?"

"Will you be at the château?"

"Yes."

"Then you'll see me," Juliana said as she rose.

Jacques shaded his eyes from the sun as he looked up at her. "You're not going to let me seduce you, are you?"

"No."

"There's not even a little chance?"

"Not even a little one."

He sighed. "Then I suppose I'll have to settle for mere friendship."

"'Friendship is Love without his wings.'"

"Wordsworth?" Jacques asked.

"Byron." Juliana laughed as she leaned over and kissed his forehead. "I'll see you later." With a smile that charmed the man, she tucked the book under her arm and headed back through the garden.

Jacques watched her until she was out of sight, then shook his head. A lot of what he'd said to her was teasing. But then again, some of it wasn't. If his cousin couldn't see what was right under his nose, he was a blind man.

Juliana walked around the house until she found a door she knew and went in. The butler was just passing through the foyer. "Marcel! I'm glad you're here. Have you seen my sister-in-law?"

"I believe she's still in her room."

"Still in her room?" she asked in surprise as she looked at her watch again. That was completely unlike Sara. "Can you tell me how to get there?"

"It's up the stairs and down the same hall as yours, seventh door on the left."

"Thank you." She ran up the steps and walked quickly down the hall to the seventh door. "Sara?" she called quietly, "are you in there?"

"Come on in, Juliana."

She opened the door a little and looked inside. Sara was sitting propped up in bed with a small writing table over her lap. "What are you doing still in bed?" she asked in concern as she went the rest of the way into the room and perched on the edge of the bed.

"I'm just not feeling very well."

"Do you need a doctor?"

"Oh, no, it's nothing serious. I just feel a little queasy when I'm up, but not really tired enough to sleep when

I'm down. I thought this was as good a time as any to catch up on my correspondence."

Juliana wasn't convinced. "Are you sure you're all right?"

"I'm sure, I'm sure. You worry too much. So does Brian."

"It's a family trait."

"I know. That's why I didn't say anything to him this morning before he left. Now forget about me. What have you been doing with your morning?"

Juliana took the book from under her arm and set it on the bedside table. "Sitting under a tree reading."

"With Alain?"

"No. Jacques."

"He's back?"

"Oh, yes. He's really very charming."

"I'm sure he'd agree with you."

Juliana smiled. "I'm sure he would, too. Lack of self-esteem isn't one of his more obvious faults."

"I could tell. Do you know what time it is?"

"Nearly noon."

"I suppose I should get up. Brian will no doubt be back any minute."

"You look awfully pale." Juliana touched the back of her hand to Sara's forehead and then her cheeks. "You don't seem to have a fever."

Sara removed Juliana's hand and held it in her own. "Stop fussing. I'm sure it's nothing more than a slight case of the flu. Go downstairs and have some lunch."

"Can I bring you anything? Some broth, perhaps? Something to drink?"

"No. I think I'll just leave my stomach comfortably empty for now."

Juliana picked up the book and headed for the door, but stopped halfway there and turned around. "Sara, do you think you could be pregnant?"

Sara looked at her in surprise. "Pregnant?" She shook her head. "I doubt it. We've tried for ten years to have a baby and haven't been able to. I'd be more than a little surprised if that's what this is."

"Maybe you should consider seeing a doctor after all. Just to be sure."

Sara had hoped so many times before and had been disappointed again and again. She wasn't going to put herself through that ever again. "No. I'll be fine in a few days."

Juliana knew better than to push. Sara could be very determined at times, and this was one of those times.

"Will you stop looking so worried and go eat?"

Juliana looked at her for a moment longer. "All right, but I'll be back in a little while." She went down the hall to her own room and saw that someone had already been there and made the bed. The hat that she'd lost in the woods was on top of the bedspread. Walking straight through to the bathroom, she washed her hands and straightened herself up, and was about to change her clothes when there was a knock on her door. She answered it and found the maid standing there.

"Hello, Yvette."

The maid wasn't used to being greeted in such a friendly fashion. "Hello. I've come to tell you that the

Duc is waiting for you in the dining room," she said in English.

"I was just going to change."

"Lunch is casual."

"So I'm all right the way I am?"

"Oh, yes. You're just fine."

She didn't feel quite right about it. There was something about this place that seemed to require formal dress for all meals, but taking the maid at her word, Juliana followed the woman down the stairs and to the dining room.

Alain was seated at the head of the table reading a newspaper. There were two other places set. Just as had been the case the night before, a servant stood behind each chair that was expected to be occupied.

The Duc folded his paper and rose as Juliana entered. "How is Byron?"

"As wonderfully melodramatic as ever," she said as she took the seat to his left. "And judging from your cousin's reaction, quite a potent sedative."

Alain smiled. "Don't mind Jacques. His idea of fine poetry usually begins and ends with 'Roses are red, violets are blue.' Is your sister-in-law going to be having lunch with us?"

"No. She's not feeling very well."

"I hope it's nothing serious."

"She says not." Juliana looked down the length of the dining-room table. "I noticed a small table on the patio last night. How would you feel about eating outside?"

"You don't like the dining room?"

"It's magnificent. But it's more like a dining hall."

"And you prefer something smaller."

Her eyes met his. "Would you mind?"

"You're my guest. If that would make you more comfortable, then that's what we'll do." He spoke to one of the servants in French, then pulled out Juliana's chair and led her through the doors to the patio and seated her at the table there with her back to the sun.

"Better?" he asked as he sat beside her.

A smile touched her mouth. "Much. Thank you."

"What else don't you like about my home?"

Juliana looked at him in surprise. "I love your home."

"But?"

Juliana shook her head. "I think it's the most beautiful place I've ever seen."

"But?"

She looked into his eyes. "Do you really want my honest opinion?"

"Believe me, Juliana, I wouldn't have asked you for it if I didn't."

"Well, all right. Here goes. Everything in the château is so old and valuable and historically significant that it makes one almost afraid to touch anything. And then there are the rooms themselves. They're of such huge proportions that they can be a bit, well...off-putting. I know you can't change some things because Marie Antoinette slept here or Napoleon sat there, but I'd love to see a wing added with overstuffed chairs and couches, and tables with some scratches on them that a person would feel safe propping his feet up on."

"I see." He seemed more amused than offended. "Tell me," he asked as the soup was served, "do you have your own home in Wisconsin?"

"Yes." She smiled as she thought about it. "It's actually more like a cottage than a house, and it's right on the shore of Lake Michigan."

"You're obviously very fond of it."

"Very."

"Do you work?"

"Yes."

"At what?"

"I design gardens for people, and sometimes the landscaping for their property."

"What an unusual job for a woman. What made you choose something like that?"

"I've always enjoyed working with flowers and colors. I also like the challenge of creating something beautiful out of nothing. And I like being outside."

Alain's eyes moved over her lovely face. "I've never met anyone like you."

A dimple flickered mysteriously in her cheek. "I should hope not."

"Why?"

"Well, because like everyone, I choose to think of myself as being unique and special." She ate some of the soup then turned her attention to Alain. "Now you know all about me. I'd like to know something about you."

"Such as?"

"I'm told you're involved in international banking."

"That's right."

"What exactly does that mean?"

"It means that I make loans and do business in countries other than France."

"Is this a family business?"

"You mean generational?"

Juliana nodded as she took a small sip of wine.

"No. I'm the first de Bournier in modern history to have an actual job."

"Why do you?"

"Because the money ran out and I needed some way to pay for the upkeep and taxes on this place."

"That's honest."

"Oh, you'll find that I'm nothing if not honest. I bought my first bank rather cheaply when it was in financial trouble about twelve years ago. Things mushroomed from there and now I own more than thirty banks."

"Do you enjoy the work?"

"Very much."

"Have you ever thought about having a family?"

His eyes met hers. "That's quite an abrupt change of subject, even for you."

A smile touched her mouth. "I was hoping you wouldn't notice if I just kind of slipped it in there quickly."

"I noticed."

Juliana was unrepentant. "Have you?"

Alain leaned back in his chair and studied her face. "Yes. And I've rejected the idea."

"Why?"

"Because I think one parents the way one has been parented, and I wouldn't want to do that to a child."

"What if you happen to fall in love with a woman who wants children?"

"I won't."

"How can you be sure?"

"I won't allow it to happen."

Juliana looked at her wine, trying very hard not to let him see how his words hurt her.

Alain cupped her chin in his hand and turned her face toward his. "Juliana, you made it clear last night that you have some romantic notion of me as your destiny. That just isn't so, and the sooner you realize that, the happier you'll be."

"I can't help what I feel."

He looked deeply into her eyes—eyes that he knew even now would haunt him for the rest of his life. It would be so easy for a man to fall in love with her. So very easy. Their faces were only inches apart. He could feel her sweet breath on his face.

"Juliana . . ." he said softly.

She touched her fingers to his lips to silence him and leaned closer.

A servant stepped onto the patio and cleared his throat. "Excuse me for interrupting, but the rest of the Sheridan family has arrived."

Neither Juliana nor Alain moved for a moment. Their eyes remained locked. Then Alain rose and held out his hand. Juliana put hers in it and rose also.

Both walked from the patio without speaking.

Chapter Four

When they got to the front door, three limousines had already unloaded their passengers and people filled the driveway. Alain looked at them in amazement. "All of these people are your family?"

Juliana smiled. "Every last one of them." She pointed to a tall man talking to one of the drivers. "That's my brother Jack. The woman next to him is his wife, Betsy, and the four children arguing over there belong to them. Then there's my brother David and his wife, Pam, and their three children. The one with the guitar is my brother Shaun and the one next to him is Tim. They're both in college. The man in the suit is my brother Matthew, who is, you'll be interested to know, president of a bank in Chicago."

"He's young for that kind of responsibility."

Juliana looked at the Frenchman with a smile. "He's not much younger than you are."

"I guess I just feel older. Decades older." He shook his head as he looked at the crowd that had descended on his home. "I've never in my life seen a family this large."

"Isn't it wonderful?"

"Juliana!" Tim yelled as soon as he saw her.

She ran into his arms and was lifted off her feet and whirled around. Then it was Matthew's turn, and then Shaun's.

"What are you all doing getting here at the same time?" she asked the crowd in general as she stood with her arm around Jack's waist.

Matthew took his briefcase out of the limousine. "We knew we were all going to have to leave out of New York anyway, so we just decided to meet there and take the same plane to Paris."

"That must have been some flight."

Jack's wife, Betsy, rolled her eyes. "Let's just say that the flight attendants looked a little dazed when we landed."

"I think I heard one of them say something about taking early retirement," Shaun said as he set his guitar case on the ground. "Where's Brian? He's supposed to be here already."

"He had some errands to run," Juliana told him, "but he should be back any minute. Sara's here."

Two children ran past them, yelling delightedly while another one chased them.

Juliana saw Alain still standing in the doorway talking to Marcel. "Come on," she said to her family, "there's someone I'd like you to meet." She walked with all of them toward the Frenchman. "I've already told Alain who all of you are. Now I'd like to introduce you to him. This is our host, the Duc de Bournier."

Alain shook hands with all of them. He was perfectly polite but the wall that seemed to slip whenever they were alone together was firmly back in place. "Welcome. I hope you will all make yourselves at home." He turned to the butler who was standing in the doorway behind him. "Marcel, please see that everyone is shown to their rooms."

"Yes, sir."

His eyes met Juliana's. "I'll leave you alone with your family for a time. I'm sure you have a lot of catching up to do." With the stiff bow that she was becoming used to, Alain turned and went back into the house.

Juliana watched him leave and nearly followed him, but Matthew caught her arm. "Well, J.J., I haven't seen you for more than six months. What's been going on in your life?"

She gazed at the empty doorway for a moment longer, then turned to her brother. "Just the usual. Work, work and more work."

"So business is good?"

"Very."

Two of the children raced past them—or tried to. Matthew bent low to wrap his arms around their waists and lifted one on either side of him. "Hey, guys, I know you've been cooped up for a long time, but don't get crazy. Running is fine outside but not inside. Understand?"

One of the little boys, Bobby, grinned, flashing the Sheridan family dimples. "Sure, Uncle Matt."

"Good." He set them back on the ground. "Go ye and sin no more."

Pam walked past Matt and touched his arm. "In your dreams. But thanks for the effort. I'd better follow them to try to mitigate the damage."

Servants had come out to help with the luggage, but the men still carried what they could into the house themselves.

"You'd better go on up with the others, Matt," Juliana suggested. "Believe me when I tell you that you'll never find your room on your own."

"That big, eh?"

"And then some."

"Pretty impressive," he said as he looked around approvingly. "I could live here."

Shaun walked past with his guitar. "Are you kidding? Napoleon's Grande Armée could have lived here and not filled the place up."

Matthew laughed as he kissed Juliana on the forehead. "See you in a few minutes."

The noise of everyone talking and laughing as they went up the stairs was friendly and warming. It made Juliana smile. And then it grew quiet again as they all found their rooms. Sara came down the steps smiling.

"They all came at once," Juliana told her. "Can you believe that?"

"I know. I was just accosted in the hall. Do you think we could get something cool to drink and find a nice, quiet place to sit?"

"You've spent the entire morning in bed and now you want to sit? Are you sure you're all right, Sara?"

"No lectures, please. You forget that I come from a family of two. I have to gear up for all of this."

"Have we been that hard to get used to?"

"It's been ten years, and I have to say quite frankly that it has been. You're all so full of energy and life. It's exhausting beyond words."

Juliana put her arm around Sara's waist as they walked through the foyer. "And you've loved every minute of it."

Sara smiled. "You know how I feel about your family. Exhausting or not, I wouldn't trade one of you."

Marcel walked past them with two maids in tow. A strand of his usually immaculate gray hair was actually out of place.

Sara, smiling irrepressibly, waited until they were out of earshot and then leaned toward Juliana. "Do you think he's going to hand in his resignation after this?" she whispered.

Juliana felt badly. Out of friendship for her father, Alain had thrown his house open to a huge family that he didn't even know. Until they departed, his entire life, and that of the people who worked for him, was going to be in turmoil. He couldn't possibly have expected it.

The two women went through a sitting room and out the doors to a patio to sit in the warm sunshine. Sara studied her sister-in-law's thoughtful face closely. "What's wrong?"

Juliana looked at her in surprise. "Nothing. Why?"

"You look so far away?"

"Just daydreaming. You should be used to that after all these years."

"I am. But this is a different look."

Juliana took a deep breath as she gazed out over the grounds. "A different look because it's a different daydream, I guess." She was silent for a few minutes. "Sara, how did you know you were in love with Brian?"

"What do you mean?"

"How did you feel? What was it that told you that Brian was the right one?"

"Oh, Juliana, that's a difficult question, and I don't really have an answer. I just looked at him one day and knew. I can't explain the whys and hows."

Juliana was silent.

"Is there someone in your life that you're trying to make up your mind about?"

"There's no need to make up my mind. I'm sure he's the one. I was sure the first moment I saw him."

"Then what's the problem?"

"One of them is that he doesn't know if I'm the one for him. And this isn't something I can convince him of. It's something he has to discover on his own."

"And you're afraid he won't?"

"I think," she said slowly, "that even if he does, his logic and tendency toward solitude will talk him out of it."

"Then you'll have to accept that it isn't meant to be."

"Either that or fight for him."

"But, Juliana, going by what you've said, there's no enemy to fight."

Juliana smiled. "At this point, I almost feel as though he's the enemy."

"Do I know this man?"

"A little."

Sara looked at Juliana's profile. "It's the Duc, isn't it?"

"What makes you say that?"

"The way you looked at him last night when you met. I knew something was going on, but I didn't know what."

"I must have been really obvious. Even Brian gave me a lecture before dinner."

"That *is* pretty obvious. Men don't usually notice things like that."

Juliana smiled, but it faded after a moment and she shook her head. "Sara, I don't know what to do. I've never felt this way before. It's as though some unseen force said to me at birth that one day I would meet the man who was meant just for me, and when I did, I'd know it without question. Unfortunately that same unseen force forgot to tell Alain."

"Men are different from women in that regard, Juliana. You can't expect that kind of recognition from ordinary men, much less someone as reserved as your

Alain. But if what you feel deep in your heart is true, he'll come to understand it on his own eventually.''

"But will he act on it?"

Sara lifted her shoulders. "Only time will tell that.''

"I suppose. It's going to be hard to just sit back and wait, though.''

Sara reached out and touched her arm. "Time, in this instance is your friend, Juliana. How can he possibly know you and not love you?''

Juliana smiled softly at her sister-in-law. "You always say the right thing.''

"For all the good it's doing you at this point.''

"You've helped, believe me.''

"There's an old saying made popular by that renowned philosopher Doris Day.''

Juliana's eyes sparkled. "Doris Day? I can't wait to hear this one.''

"Que sera, sera."

"What will be will be," Juliana translated.

Sara smiled. "It sounds silly, but it's true. If you and Alain are truly meant to be together, it will happen.''

"I know," Juliana said quietly.

"And if you aren't . . .''

"I know that, too.''

"It's strange.''

"What is?''

"From the day I met you, I knew there was something different about you. You seemed to be searching for something without knowing what it was.''

"I didn't know, until yesterday.''

"But regardless of the outcome, your search is over. How many of us, if we're truly honest, can say that our search is over? Always we're wondering if we're truly living out our destiny. As much as I love your brother, I once in a great while find myself questioning what I have with him. I ask myself that age-old question, is that all there is?"

"But I've watched the two of you together. After all this time, you're still very much in love."

"We are," Sara agreed. "But I never felt that sense of recognition that you've just described. Brian and I just sort of evolved." Sara shook her head. "I'm not explaining myself well. The fact is that I wouldn't trade what I have with Brian for anything in the world."

"I know that."

"But even I, for all that my husband touts me as one of the most wonderfully logical women in the world, have my romantically whimsical moments."

"That's the difference between us," Juliana said with a smile. "The times when I'm solidly logical are mere moments. Mostly I'm an irrepressible romantic."

"There's nothing wrong with that."

"Except, as someone recently reminded me, it's the romantics in the world who get hurt. Our expectations sometimes have no basis in reality."

"It's your nature, Juliana. A person can't change his nature."

"Especially not at this late date."

Sara touched her arm again. "You'll be all right, you know. Whatever happens."

Both women fell silent.

"Did I hear you correctly earlier when you said there was more than one problem?" Sara asked.

"Umm-hmm."

"What's the other one."

Juliana looked at Sara. "My other problem is what to do if it turns out Alain *does* want me."

Sara shook her head. "You've lost me with that one."

Juliana gazed at the home behind them. "Look at all this. It's not me. I don't know if I could live here."

"Perhaps he'd be willing to live somewhere else."

"Of course he wouldn't," she said quietly. "This home has been in his family for generations. The life he's led here is the only kind of life he knows. If you've had trouble adjusting to us as a family, can you imagine what he'd go through?"

"I see what you mean."

"Maybe I should just go home after the costume ball tomorrow and not wait for the ending to my story with Alain."

"But don't you think that not knowing would be worse than knowing for sure?"

"I don't think so. At this point I feel that either way I lose."

"There you two are!" said Brian as he came out the door and kissed his wife on the cheek. "I just saw the rest of the group. They should be down in a few minutes." He sat next to Sara and looked from one woman to the other. "Why so quiet?"

"We were just talking."

"Did I interrupt?"

"No," Juliana said. "We were finished."

Sara looked at Brian and smiled. "Do you know that I love you?" she asked simply.

He looked at her curiously. "Umm-hmm. I love you, too."

"And that's all that matters."

Brian looked at his sister suspiciously. "Boy, I'd like to be a bug on the wall sometimes when you two talk."

"You wouldn't understand a word we said," Juliana told him with an affectionate smile.

"Which is no reflection on you personally," Sara said. "Just men in general."

"I think I'm offended."

"Don't be." Sara looped her arm through his. "I'll tell you about my end of the conversation later."

Matt, Tim and Shaun came onto the patio and sank onto the chairs. "Why does sitting on a seat in a plane for hours on end wear people out so much?" asked Tim. "I'm beat."

To anyone watching the group on the porch, the four men and Juliana were obviously related. Their hair was thick and unruly with the same hint of red; their eyes were green; their smiles quick and white, and there was an unspoken intimacy among them.

"Who brought the football?" Juliana asked.

"I was elected equipment manager," Tim said.

Alain walked onto the patio. "I'm having refreshments served shortly. And I thought that since it's such a lovely evening outside," he said as he looked directly at Juliana, "we would have dinner on the patio."

The expression in Juliana's eyes was warmly grateful. "That sounds nice."

"I thought you'd like that." He sat across from Matthew. "Your sister tells me that you're involved in banking."

Matt grinned at him. "I'm glad you brought that up. You're something of a legend in my circles and I would thoroughly enjoy talking to you about business."

At that moment, the rest of the Sheridans came out onto the patio and chaos reigned. Voices crossed over each other, children giggled, adults laughed and everyone was happy.

Juliana sat quietly and watched everyone, but her gaze invariably came back to Alain. He listened politely to Matt, making occasional comments. He rarely smiled and never laughed, but he seemed truly interested with what her brother was saying and wasn't at all condescending.

He seemed to sense that she was watching him and turned his head. Their eyes met and held. Without changing his expression, Alain answered a question Matt had asked while still looking at her, then turned back to her brother.

Sara leaned toward Juliana. "He's not as aloof as he'd like everyone to think. At least not when it comes to you."

"So it would appear." She got to her feet. "I'm going to go upstairs to change before dinner. I've had on the same clothes since dawn."

Juliana was learning her way around. She found her room on the first try, took a shower and put on a flowing white dress with a wide royal-blue belt.

The afternoon had flown by and night was falling fast. She opened the balcony doors and smiled quietly when she heard the faint sound of Shaun's guitar and the hum of voices.

Slipping on her sandals, Juliana ran back downstairs and onto the patio. Shaun and Tim, who'd discovered the music of the sixties and seventies, were harmonizing on an old song. As soon as Tim saw her, he waved her over to sit on his lap and her high clear voice joined theirs.

As the final notes drifted into silence, a single pair of hands began clapping. "I still say you kids could take your act on the road."

Juliana looked up and beamed at the man who'd been watching unnoticed on the patio. "Dad!" she cried, leaping up and running into his arms. "What are you doing here?"

"I couldn't stand the thought that you were all here and I was in Paris. I told your mother a tall tale, for which I'm going to have to apologize profusely tomorrow night, and headed out here to see you for a few minutes. Alain told me everyone had arrived, so here I am."

Alain, who'd been standing behind the ambassador, crossed the patio to where he'd left a drink, picked it up, leaned his shoulder against a pillar and watched while Charles Sheridan's children and grandchildren crowded around him, all talking at once.

Picking up a small granddaughter, Charles walked over to a swinging chair and sat down with her on his lap. "Well," he asked the group in general, "are we all set with costumes for tomorrow?"

"We're ready," Brian said. "What are you telling Mom?"

"Thanks to Alain," he said as he looked at the man standing apart from the group, "she thinks she's coming to your basic costume ball. She has no idea it's an anniversary party or that any of you are going to be here."

Juliana smiled and touched his shoulder. "I bet it's been hard for you to keep this from her."

He shook his gray head. "You wouldn't believe how many times I've nearly broken down and told her. She misses all of you so much. But tomorrow night when she finally sees all of you together, the expression on her face is going to be worth the secrecy."

Alain looked at his watch. "Sir, it's time for you to leave now."

The ambassador glanced at his watch as well. "I suppose so. I knew I was only going to have a few minutes, but I just couldn't resist." Rising to his feet, he set his granddaughter on the ground and took Juliana's hand in his. "Have a fun evening. I'll see you all tomorrow." He looked at his daughter. "J.J., why don't you walk me out to the car?"

They were halfway down the hall when she looked up at him, her green eyes worried. Her father was a little too serious. "Is something wrong?"

"Wrong? Not at all. Why?"

"You seem preoccupied."

"Oh, it's just business. Sometimes I'm required to be more diplomatic than I feel."

"Did you have a rough day?"

"You could say that. There are times when the world is not a very pleasant place to live. But I'm feeling much better now that I've seen you and your brothers. Just the pick-me-up I needed."

"Good."

He kissed the top of her head. "Thanks, honey." He climbed into the back seat of his limousine.

"Dad, may I ask you something?"

"Of course."

"How did you come to know Alain?"

"Nothing mysterious. He arranged some financing through his banks to secure the release of hostages."

"The ones that came home last year?"

"Yes. He lost his shirt, but I've never heard a complaint."

"You like him, don't you?"

"Very much. He's a fine young man." The ambassador looked at his only daughter curiously. "Why the interest?"

"I was just wondering." She sounded innocent enough. Perhaps a little too innocent.

"You have to understand that the fact that I like Alain doesn't mean that I'd care to see you get involved with him."

"Why not?"

"You're such different people. Since the day you were born, you've pulsed with emotion. Alain never displays any emotion at all. It's as though he's never happy, but never sad, either. He never exposes himself emotionally to anyone."

"How long have you known him?"

"Since I came to France two years ago. Don't misunderstand, Juliana. Alain de Bournier is a man of great integrity. I trust him completely."

"But not with me."

He shook his head. "I'm sorry, but no, not with you."

He closed his door and he pressed a button that wound down his window.

"I'm not too late with the warning, am I?" he asked.

Juliana smiled at him. "I don't know yet."

"If you need to talk, you know where I am."

She nodded.

"Good night, J.J. I'll see you tomorrow night."

"All right." She kissed his cheek, then stood in the driveway waving as the car pulled out and disappeared into the distance.

She stood there for a long time after everything was quiet. The lights from the château spilled onto the driveway. The moon hung low in the sky.

When she finally turned to go back inside, she found Alain standing in the doorway watching her.

Chapter Five

Juliana stood still for a moment, then walked toward him. "Have you been standing there long?"

"No. Would it matter if I had?"

"Probably not." They walked through the foyer. "My father thinks very highly of you."

"It's mutual. Why does your family call you J.J.?"

"It's their shorthand for Juliana Justine."

A little girl came running down the hall as she looked over her shoulder and crashed right into her aunt. Juliana laughed as she scooped her up into her arms. "Who are you running from, Kari?"

"Bobby."

At that moment, Bobby came tearing around the corner, but when he saw Kari with the two adults, he turned around and ran in the opposite direction.

Kari leaned back so she could look at Juliana. "Will you take me to see the fountain? Mommie said I can't go there by myself. I might fall in."

"Of course." She looked at Alain. "Would you like to go with us?"

He seemed to almost say yes. Almost, but not quite. "I don't think so."

"Uncle Tim will." Kari climbed out of Juliana's arms and ran down the hall. "I'll ask."

A moment later, when Juliana stepped onto the patio, Tim was already standing at the ready, Kari's hand in his. Juliana took Kari's other hand and the three of them walked down the steps and onto the lawn. Juliana took off her sandals as she walked and carried them by their straps in her free hand. Much to Kari's delight, Juliana and Tim counted to three and then swung her high in the air between them. Every few steps they'd swing her again.

Alain watched the three of them. It was a picture from a charmingly old-fashioned postcard.

Sara quietly studied the Frenchman and smiled to herself when she saw that his eyes were riveted on Juliana's disappearing figure. She had no way of knowing what was going on in his mind, but it was obvious to her that he was affected by Juliana's presence. And apparently also her absence. If she'd had to put a label on Alain's expression, she would have called it wistful. Odd in a man so apparently emotionless.

By the time Juliana, Tim and Kari returned, dinner was being served. Instead of the many courses of the night before, the cook had cut things back and had only the main meal, dessert and coffee. The Sheridans laughed and talked about everything from personal anecdotes to politics to literature. Juliana was a bit more quiet than usual. Her eyes kept going to Alain's expressionless face. She'd never met anyone who was more effective at hiding his thoughts.

Everyone was tired after the long trip and the children had been ready for bed for ages, so it wasn't long after dinner that the group broke up. Alain and Juliana looked at each other across the suddenly silent patio.

"As I told you earlier," Alain said, "you have a large family."

"But a nice one."

"If you happen to like large families."

"I do. You will, too, when you've had a chance to get to know them better."

"I'm sure I will."

Juliana didn't believe him for a second. That was nothing more than his good manners speaking.

Alain got to his feet. "There are some things I'd like to do. Would you mind if I left you to your own devices for the rest of the evening?"

Juliana looked up at him with a smile that touched her eyes. "Of course not. You've already been more than generous with your time."

"Good night, then. I may not see you tomorrow. At least not until the ball."

"Work?"

"A lot of it."

Her eyes met and held his. "I'm sorry," she said quietly. "Good night, Alain."

He started to say something else, but changed his mind and turned away from her.

Juliana leaned her head against the back of her chair and gazed at the sky. Stars filled the blackness. The moon was there, in all of its bold size, its illumination dimmed by clouds scudding in front of it.

It was much too beautiful a night to stay there. Getting up, she left the patio and stepped onto the grass. After walking just a few steps, she took off her sandals and let her toes sink into the dewy green carpet.

It was late and dark and she was very much alone, but Juliana didn't mind. She felt completely safe. Crossing the grounds, walking slowly, she went into the forest, not toward the stream this time, but along a path lined with trees that went on and on, but then, with surprising suddenness opened into rolling hills.

She heard the horse before she saw it. Its hooves were thundering against the earth, faster and faster, closer and closer. She gasped and turned toward the sound. The animal seemed to burst from the forest all at once, not fifty feet from where she was standing, and aimed straight at her.

Juliana didn't move. She couldn't. It was as though her feet were frozen to the earth.

The horse suddenly stopped and reared, its flailing hooves coming within just a few feet of her.

Alain sat on he horse's back, the tense muscles of his forearms evident in the moonlight as he got the horse under control. When he was still, he stroked the animal's great neck to calm him down. His dark eyes flashed angrily at Juliana. "What in the hell are you doing out here?"

Juliana's heart finally started beating again. "I went for a walk."

"You have no business being out here alone so far from the château this late at night."

"There's nothing here to hurt me." She eyed the horse. "At least there wasn't."

"You're lucky I saw you."

She moved closer to the horse who was still straining against his bit, his nostrils flaring. "Do you always ride like that?" she asked as she rested her hand soothingly against the animal's arched neck.

"How I ride is none of your business." He held out his hand to her. "Come. I'll take you back to the house."

"I don't want to go back."

"What are you going to do out here?"

"Walk. Explore a little."

He seemed undecided about what to do. "I can't leave you here alone."

"Of course you can. You're my host, not my keeper."

"I'm responsible for you."

Her eyes met his in the moonlight. "No one is responsible for me but me. You go ahead and finish your ride and I'll finish my walk."

She turned and would have walked away from him, but Alain moved his horse into position and blocked her path. "Let's ride together."

"I really don't..."

Alain got down from the horse, and without saying another word, put his hands at her waist and lifted Juliana onto the saddle, then climbed up behind her. Her back was against his chest as she turned her head to one side and looked up at him. "Now what do you intend to do?"

His eyes met hers, but instead of answering, he kneed his horse and headed up the hill. The angle at which they were riding forced her even more closely against his chest.

Alain inhaled the sweet fragrance of her hair as it brushed against his chin. He felt the warmth of her body as it touched his. His own body stirred in response.

Juliana closed her eyes to shut out everything but what she was feeling as his strong arms circled her to hold the reins. The warmth from his body soaked through her blouse and warmed her. Despite the wind moving her hair, she could feel his breath. Her skin tingled with a remarkable and very delicious sensitivity.

When they got to the top of the hill, Alain stopped the horse, climbed down and put his hands at Juliana's waist to lift her to the ground. Their eyes were locked as he slowly slid her body past his. She found it difficult to breathe. "Why are we stopping here?" she finally managed to ask.

"Because this is where I was headed when I almost rode into you."

"Rode over me," she corrected.

A corner of his mouth lifted and a groove in his cheek deepened. "Either way, it would have hurt." His hands dropped to his sides. Leaving the horse untethered to graze on the sweet grass, he walked toward a lone tree and sat under it, his back leaning against the trunk.

Juliana joined him on the ground, near, but not near enough to touch. The moon hung low in the sky. She could see the lights of the château through the tops of the trees.

"This tree," he said quietly, "is probably five hundred years old. It's seen everyone who's ever come and gone. It's stood here through royalty and revolution, peace and war. I wonder what it would have to tell if it could talk?"

Juliana's eyes rested on his profile.

Alain turned his head as though sensing that she was looking at him and met her gaze. "What are you thinking?"

"You seem so coldly logical. I never expected to hear you say anything whimsical."

"You're apparently rubbing off on me."

"And after only a day. Think how you'll be after an entire week in my company."

"Fortunately for me, I'm leaving here after tomorrow night's ball."

Juliana tried not to show him how much his words had distressed her. "For how long?"

"A month. Perhaps longer."

"So I won't see you again after tomorrow?"

"I wouldn't think so."

Her throat grew tight. "I see. I imagine you have to travel a lot in your business."

"I'm not leaving on business. I'm leaving because of you."

Her eyes searched his. "Me?"

"Yes." He shook his head. "There's something about you. I have this uneasy feeling that you're going to turn my world upside down and I like my world exactly as it is."

"You've never tried anything else."

"Nor do I wish to."

Juliana looked toward the château.

Alain's eyes lingered on the lovely line of her face. "How much have you slept in the past three days?"

"I don't know," Juliana said as she delicately lifted her shoulders. "Four, maybe five hours."

"You must be exhausted."

"I just have a hard time sleeping when things around me are new. Like a child, I guess, I'm afraid I'll miss something."

Alain lay back on the grass, his hands behind his head, and gazed at the sky. Everything was silent except for the comforting night noises that belonged there.

"It's so peaceful," Juliana said in a whisper. "Is that why you come here?"

"Yes."

"I have a place like this at home. It's a spot high on some rocks overlooking Lake Michigan. You'd like it there."

"Juliana?"

She looked down at him.

"Come here."

"What?"

"I said come here. Stop talking, lie down and put your head on my shoulder."

"I . . ."

"Shhhh."

Juliana lay next to him, on her back, and rested her head on his shoulder. Alain curved his arm around her and sighed. "Are you cold?"

"No."

The scent of him filled her senses. Her entire body filled with an aching longing unlike anything she'd ever felt before, but she lay absolutely still.

"Just push everything from your mind except this place," Alain said softly, his mouth just above her ear.

Juliana looked at the stars. Without her realizing it, though, her eyes slowly drifted closed. Her senses were full of the man lying beside her, his arm touching her, her cheek against the fabric of his shirt. A wonderful drowsiness filled her limbs, making them heavy. The last thing she intended to do was to fall asleep, but she did. Within minutes.

Alain listened to her deep even breath and smiled slightly. Her long days and nights had finally caught up with her.

She turned onto her side so that her cheek was against his chest and her arm rested lightly across his stomach. Her head was right under his chin. Without realizing he was doing it, Alain gently rubbed his cheek against the curling softness of her hair. He wanted to hold her and protect her, and he didn't know why. Until two days ago, he hadn't even known she existed. Why should anything about her matter to him?

She made him feel so uneasy.

Juliana sighed and moved closer, snuggling against his side. Her soft breath touched his throat.

"God," he whispered hoarsely as his arm tightened around her, holding her closer. He buried his lips in her silky hair.

For hours they lay like that. Alain was unwilling to wake her from what little sleep she took, but was unable to sleep himself. He stared at the sky, completely aware of even the slightest movement of the woman he held; of every breath she took. She filled his thoughts to the exclusion of everything else.

Juliana awakened. It was a slow, wonderful awakening as she grew to awareness that she was outside, but warm and safe. She could hear Alain's heart beating beneath her ear.

She raised her head and turned more onto her stomach so that she could look at him. It was still dark, but she could see his eyes looking into hers. Without saying anything, she kissed the corner of his mouth, then drew back and looked into his eyes again. He gazed back at her unblinkingly.

She slowly leaned forward again and lightly touched her lips to his.

"Juliana, this..."

"Please, don't talk," she whispered against his mouth. "Just kiss me."

With a groan, Alain's arms wrapped around her, pulling her body on top of his. His fingers tangled in her hair as he pressed her lips to his, hard at first, with a desire he'd repressed since the moment he'd seen her, and then more tenderly as the kiss grew deeper. He explored every corner of her mouth, and she explored his, running her tongue along his strong white teeth. Alain rolled over and gently laid Juliana on her back. For a long time, in utter silence, he gazed into her eyes. "What are you doing to me, Juliana?" he asked softly.

"I love you."

He kissed the corners of her mouth, then looked into her eyes again. "You don't know me. If you did, you wouldn't feel what you think you're feeling."

Her eyes never left his. "I can't explain to you how I know what I know. But our being together is right. Can't you see that? Can't you feel it?"

"What I feel is what any man in his right mind would feel while holding you in his arms. I want to make love to you, but I don't want to love you."

Juliana trailed her fingers down his beard-roughened cheek. "Have you ever loved anyone?"

"Not the way you do. And not the way you want me to; the way you need me to." He rolled away from her and got to his feet. Holding out his hand, he gazed at her in the moonlight. "I'd better take you back."

In silence, she put her hand in his.

Alain didn't release her right away, but cupped her chin in his hand and looked into her moist eyes. "Oh, Juliana Sheridan," he said softly, "I wish, for both our sakes, that I was a different kind of man."

"But you aren't, and I don't wish you were any way other than the way you are."

He rested his lips against her forehead, then stepped away from her. "Come on."

Alain lifted her onto the horse that grazed nearby, then climbed up behind her. Slowly and in silence, they rode down the hill and through the forest. He stopped in front of the château and held Juliana's hand as she slipped to the ground. Still holding her hand, he looked down at her. "I'm sorry," he said quietly.

The sun had just started to rise. To his amazement, Juliana's soft green eyes held a smile in their depths. "Don't be. You're going to change your mind, you know."

He shook his head as his eyes moved over her face. "You're the most amazing woman. You have such strong convictions."

"Not about everything."

"Just about us?"

"I'm not wrong. You are."

"You're going to get hurt."

"Perhaps."

He released her hand, but sat looking at her for a moment longer before riding toward the stables.

Juliana watched until he was out of sight, then turned and went into the château and up the stairs to her room.

With her clothes on, she lay on the bed and stared unseeingly at the ceiling, full of conflicting emotions and unable to sort them out into anything that made sense.

All she knew was what she felt in her heart, and she wouldn't accept the possibility that she was wrong. This wasn't some fantasy. This was her life.

* * *

When Alain reached the stables, he unsaddled his horse and began brushing him down.

"Hello, cousin."

He looked up to find Jacques standing in the doorway. "What are you doing here at this hour?"

"I've been here for quite a while. I came looking for Juliana last night and discovered that you were both missing. I saw you drop her off at the château just now."

Alain went on with his brushing.

"She's a lovely woman."

"Yes, she is."

"Rather fragile."

Alain didn't say anything.

"I'd hate to see anything happen to her."

"Such as?"

Jacques walked farther into the stables and leaned against one of the stall gates. "Such as setting her heart on a man who hasn't got one."

Alain finished brushing the horse and led it into a stall, latching the gate after it. "I agree with you."

Jacques looked at his cousin in undisguised amazement. "You do?"

"Yes. She's got some odd ideas about me that I can't seem to talk her out of."

"So what are you going to do about it?"

"Well, I can't very well leave before my own party, but I've made arrangements to be out of the country beginning the morning after. I plan to be away until she's safely back in the United States."

"Do you think that's enough?"

"It's all that's left. I've tried telling her, in so many words, what a bastard I am, but she simply doesn't want to believe it. I even told her why I'm leaving town."

Jacques looked at Alain with new respect. "You really care about her, don't you?"

"Don't you start on me. I've had enough of that for one evening."

"I'm serious. She's getting to you, isn't she?"

Alain dragged his fingers through his hair. "Yes," he said softly. "She's getting to me. She's beautiful. She's gentle. To look at her is to want to make love to her. And she thinks she's in love with me. That's a pretty hard combination to resist."

"But you did resist, didn't you? Tonight when you were with her?"

"Not that it's any of your business, but yes, I did."

Jacques moved away from the stall gate. "Well, cousin, this is a side of you I've never seen before."

"Is Juliana the reason you waited here all through the night to talk to me?"

Jacques fell into step beside his cousin. "Yes. I was worried."

"You realize, of course, that she's not for you, either, don't you?"

"Oh, yes. Her interest in me is strictly as a friend she can read Byron with."

"Make sure you keep it that way. I may not be able to commit myself to a woman, but you commit yourself to entirely too many of them."

Jacques smiled. "That's true."

The two cousins, who had never been particularly good friends, suddenly found themselves being quite companionable. As they approached the château, Alain glanced over at Jacques. "You've had a long night. Instead of driving all the way home, you might as well just stay here."

"Thanks. I appreciate it."

"Just remember what I said about Juliana. She's hands-off for both of us."

"That's fair."

The two parted at the door to the château. Jacques went inside and to the room he used whenever he stayed. Alain remained outside. Sitting in a chair on the patio, he watched the sun rise the rest of the way. There was no point in trying to sleep. He knew he'd never be able to.

His mind kept saying Juliana's name over and over again, almost like a mantra.

An image of her face kept swimming into view.

He could still feel the warmth of her lips where they'd touched his.

He could still feel her hair beneath his fingertips and smell the fresh scent of her skin.

Alain sighed and leaned his head against the back of the chair.

He'd never wanted a woman as much as he wanted Juliana. But wanting a woman wasn't love. And she was a woman who should be loved, above anything else.

Chapter Six

The family had split into two teams. Juliana raced out from the pack. "Over here, Tim!"

Tim spotted her, crooked his arm and sent the football flying over everyone else's head, straight into Juliana's arms. She ran across the lawn with the other team in full pursuit of her. Shaun caught her first, tackling her by wrapping his arms around her and whirling her in the air before setting her back on her feet. "Gotcha, kiddo."

Juliana wrinkled her nose at him. "This time. But the game's not over yet, buster."

He grinned at her. "But it will be soon, and you're going to lose."

Narrowing her eyes with renewed determination, Juliana walked over to Brian, Tim, Sara and Pam. "We're in big trouble. Let's huddle."

Both Jacques and Alain watched from Alain's office inside the château.

"What is it about large American families that drives them to play touch football?" Jacques asked. "It must be some kind of strange custom they have. Either that or it's something in their genes. They actually seem to enjoy it."

Alain was silent as he watched the game in progress. The huddle broke up. Shaun had the ball. He faked a pass to Jack and started to run with the ball, but Juliana had guessed that that was what he intended to do and grabbed him before he'd made it ten feet.

Alain's smile flashed. "She's not bad."

"Not bad?" Jacques said. "She's terrific. Who would have guessed that someone that feminine could catch a ball like a boy and run that fast?"

Alain watched Juliana in silence, then moved away from the window and went to his desk.

"Don't you want to join them?" Jacques asked, turning and looking at his cousin.

"No."

"I think I will."

"You've never played football in your life."

"Not to play. To watch."

"If that's what you like, then by all means do so."

Jacques started to say something else, but Alain was already reading his mail. He quietly left the room and closed the door behind him.

Alain stared blindly at the sheet of paper in front of him. After a minute he put it down with a sigh, rubbed his eyes and left his office.

When Jacques got downstairs, the game was over and the players were leaving the field, some a little the worse for wear. Brian had his arm around Sara's shoulders, more so she could support him than in affection. "I'm getting too old for this," he groaned.

"We're all getting too old for this."

"Maybe we should take up horseshoes."

"Or shuffleboard."

Jacques walked out on the lawn and met Juliana as she walked toward the château. "You seem to have held up a little better than your brother."

"Which one?"

"Brian."

Juliana smiled. "Oh, he's fine. He just likes the sympathy Sara gives him."

"She didn't sound too sympathetic."

"Maybe she's on to him. He does the same thing every time we play football."

Jacques shook his head. "You have a strange family."

"But likable."

"Very."

When they got to the patio, there was a cart with a pitcher of lemonade, ice and glasses. "Oh," Juliana sighed, "I've died and gone to heaven. Who thought of this?"

"Marcel probably."

SILHOUETTE GIVES YOU SIX REASONS TO CELEBRATE!

MAIL THE BALLOON TODAY!

INCLUDING:

1.
4 FREE BOOKS

2.
A LOVELY 20k GOLD ELECTROPLATED CHAIN

3.
A SURPRISE BONUS

AND MORE!

TAKE A LOOK...

Yes, become a Silhouette subscriber and the celebration goes on forever.

To begin with we'll send you:

4 new Silhouette Romance™ novels — FREE

a lovely 20k gold electroplated chain—FREE

an exciting mystery bonus—FREE

And that's not all! Special extras— Three more reasons to celebrate.

4. **FREE Home Delivery!** That's right! We'll send you 4 FREE books, and you'll be under no obligation to purchase any in the future. You may keep the books and return the accompanying statement marked cancel.

If we don't hear from you, about a month later we'll send you six additional novels to read and enjoy. If you decide to keep them, you'll pay the already low price of just $2.25* each — AND there's no extra charge for delivery! There are no hidden extras! You may cancel at any time! But as long as you wish to continue, every month we'll send you six more books, which you can purchase or return at our cost, cancelling your subscription.

5. **Free Monthly Newsletter!** It's the indispensable insiders' look at our most popular writers and their upcoming novels. Now you can have a behind-the-scenes look at the fascinating world of Silhouette! It's an added bonus you'll look forward to every month!

6. **More Surprise Gifts!** Because our home subscribers are our most valued readers, we'll be sending you additional free gifts from time to time — as a token of our appreciation.

FREE! 20k GOLD ELECTROPLATED CHAIN!

You'll love this 20k gold electroplated chain! The necklace is finely crafted with 160 double-soldered links, and is electroplate finished in genuine 20k gold. It's nearly 1/8″ wide, fully 20″ long — and has the look and feel of the real thing. "Glamorous" is the perfect word for it, and it can be yours FREE in this amazing Silhouette celebration!

SILHOUETTE ROMANCE™

FREE OFFER CARD

4 FREE BOOKS

20k GOLD ELECTROPLATED CHAIN—FREE

FREE MYSTERY BONUS

PLACE YOUR BALLOON STICKER HERE

FREE HOME DELIVERY

FREE FACT-FILLED NEWSLETTER

MORE SURPRISE GIFTS THROUGHOUT THE YEAR—FREE

YES! Please send me my four Silhouette Romance™ novels FREE, along with my 20k Electroplated Gold Chain and my free mystery gift, as explained on the opposite page. I understand that accepting these books and gifts places me under no obligation ever to buy any books. I may cancel at any time for any reason, and the free books and gifts will be mine to keep!   215 CIS HAYH (U-S-R-02/90)

NAME

(PLEASE PRINT)

ADDRESS   APT

CITY   STATE

ZIP

SILHOUETTE "NO RISK GUARANTEE"
• There's no obligation to buy — the free books and gifts remain yours to keep.
• You receive books before they're available in stores.
• You may end your subscription anytime — just by letting us know.

PRINTED IN U.S.A.

Remember! To receive your free books, chain and a surprise mystery bonus, return the postpaid card below. But don't delay.

DETACH AND MAIL CARD TODAY
If offer card has been removed, write to: Silhouette Reader Service, 901 Fuhrmann Blvd., P.O. Box 1867, Buffalo, NY 14269-1867

FILL OUT THIS POSTPAID CARD AND MAIL TODAY!

NO POSTAGE
NECESSARY
IF MAILED
IN THE
UNITED STATES

BUSINESS REPLY CARD
FIRST CLASS   PERMIT NO. 717   BUFFALO, N.Y.

Postage will be paid by addressee

SILHOUETTE BOOKS®

901 Fuhrmann Blvd.,
P.O. Box 1867
Buffalo, N.Y. 14240-9952

No sooner had his name been spoken than Marcel materialized beside them. "Is there anything I can get for you?"

Juliana kissed his cheek. "You're a wonderful man."

The butler tried hard not to smile.

"And the lemonade is all I need. Thank you for bringing it."

"You're quite welcome."

Juliana poured herself a glass and collapsed onto a chair. Tim and Jack were still on the lawn tossing the football back and forth. The little Sheridans were getting in on it, too.

"When are they going to be allowed to play?" Jacques asked.

"When they can hold their own. Of course, by that time the rest of us will be in wheelchairs."

Jacques laughed as he sat next to her. "You should start a little Sheridan training camp."

"That's what that is," she said as she inclined her head toward the ones still on the lawn.

Jacques watched for a moment. "That one little boy is pretty good."

"That's Jack, Jr."

"Jack, Jr.," he repeated. "It's hard to tell the boys apart. They all look so much alike."

Silence fell between them as they watched until Juliana finally asked the question that had been on her mind all morning. "Do you know where Alain is? I haven't seen him yet today."

"The last time I saw him he was in his office reading his mail."

"Oh."

"Why do you ask?"

"I was simply wondering."

"You sound so casual, but I get the feeling your question is anything but that."

Juliana looked at Jacques over the rim of her glass. "Are you trying to make a not-so-subtle point here?"

He shook his head. "Not at all."

"Thank you."

He stared at her for a time before speaking again. "I talked with Alain last night in the stables after he dropped you off here at the château."

Juliana held the cool glass to her warm cheek, but didn't comment.

"Don't you want to know what we talked about?"

"No."

"You surprise me."

"I apparently surprise a lot of people."

"Could it be that you don't want to know because you know you aren't going to like it?"

"Yes," she agreed, "it could very well be that. Now can we please change the subject? What kind of costume are you wearing to the ball tonight?"

"I'm coming as Beau Brummell."

"The Regency dandy?"

"The one and only."

Juliana smiled at him. "That's perfect for you."

Jacques smiled, but then his smile faded. "I think I'm insulted."

"Don't be. That's just the way you are."

"What about you?"

"I'm coming as Bernardine Eugenie Désirée Clary."

Jacques looked at her with interest. "You're coming as Napoleon's first love?"

"First, and some say really his only love."

"Josephine fans would disagree."

"I know."

"Do you already have the costume?"

"I brought it with me."

"And a mask?"

"I brought that, too. It's one of those that's attached to a stick and the wearer has to hold it to her eyes."

As she talked, Juliana was watching Kari chase one of her cousins across the lawn. When Kari got to the cinder path, her foot slipped and she landed hard on her knees and elbows. Juliana quickly set her glass down and ran to her, but Alain was already there. He kneeled next to the crying child and cuddled her on his lap, rocking her back and forth until the sobbing had eased into hiccups and sniffles. Then setting Kari in the grass, he carefully checked the scrapes, talking softly the entire time in an attempt to reassure her.

Juliana watched with a soft smile. His gentleness was no surprise to her.

She rested her hand on Alain's shoulder and he looked up at her. "She looks just the way you looked at that age, doesn't she?" he asked about Kari.

"That's what the pictures say."

"I can imagine your own daughter with the same hair, the same eyes," he said softly.

"I guess that will partly depend on my daughter's father." She kneeled next to Alain and her arm pressed lightly against his. "Well, young lady," she said as she ruffled Kari's hair, "I suppose we should find you some bandages."

Alain rose with Kari in his arms. "I know just the place."

They went to the kitchen where there was a huge woman chopping tomatoes on a cutting board, wielding the large knife like a machete. She looked up when they walked in and smiled.

"Genvieve," Alain said in English, "this is Juliana Sheridan and this," he said as he set Kari on the countertop, "is Kari Sheridan. She took a spill and needs some bandages."

The woman wiped her hands on a towel and went to a cabinet near the sink. Juliana wet a paper towel to clean the scrapes while the Frenchwoman clucked over the little girl like a mother hen. "You eat this," she said, bringing her a handful of cookies. "Everyone loves Genvieve's cookies. They'll make you smile."

Alain smiled at Kari and winked, then without another word, left the kitchen. Genvieve moved into the breach, pinching her cheeks. "What a lovely thing you are."

Juliana watched Alain's disappearing back, then still thoughtful, she cleaned Kari's scrapes and put a bandage on each knee and one on her elbow. "There you go, munchkin. All better." She turned her attention to the older woman. "Are you the magician who prepares the wonderful meals we've been eating?"

The woman positively beamed at her. "I am the Duc's chef, yes."

"I was sure it was a man."

"Ah, well, most great chefs in France are men. I'm an exception."

"I'd like to watch you work sometime, if that's all right. Perhaps I can learn a few things."

"I would be honored, Miss Sheridan." She smiled at her. "My husband said you were a pretty little thing. He was right."

"Your husband?"

"Marcel."

Juliana couldn't hide her surprise. Never had two people looked less as though they belonged together.

Genvieve laughed good-naturedly. "I know. The odd couple, yes?"

"As long as you're happy, that's all that matters."

"That's what we thought twenty years ago and it's turned out to be true."

"That's wonderful."

Kari tugged on Juliana's arm. She picked the little girl up. "I'll see you again soon, Genvieve."

"I'll look forward to it, Miss Sheridan."

"Please, call me Juliana."

"Of course." The chef was still smiling long after the two had left. It was wonderful having that family around. It made the place more like a real home.

Alain had gone back upstairs to his office. He sat behind his desk and tried to concentrate on his mail, but it was useless. Walking to the window, he stared outside. He'd known many women in his life and had even slept with some of them. And he'd loved none of them. He never even thought about them. It was as though they'd never existed, so untouched did they leave his world.

And then there was Juliana Sheridan telling him some nonsense about recognition and destiny.

It was ridiculous. A product of an overactive romantic imagination.

And yet he couldn't get her out of his mind. Her lovely face, and those bright, wonderful eyes, seemed etched into his mind, and popped up at the strangest times.

He turned abruptly and left the château. Noelle would help him to forget that face.

It was late when Juliana finally went to her room to dress for the ball. She hadn't seen Alain all day. Walking over to the portrait of his ancestor, she stood for a long time just staring at it.

So deep in her thoughts was Juliana that she jumped a foot off the ground when some knuckles fell sharply on her door. She opened it to find Sara standing there already dressed in her costume and looking stunning.

"Oh, Sara," she said with a smile. "You make a wonderful Marie Antoinette."

"As long as no one tries to behead me, I'll do just fine." She cleared her throat. "Let them eat cake! How's that?"

"Very regal—except that she never said that."

"You're kidding."

"No. It was just a nasty rumor started by the revolutionaries to make her seem as callous as possible."

"Rats. I guess I'll have to come up with a new line." She looked Juliana up and down, for the first time noticing what she was wearing. "For heaven's sake, you haven't even started to dress yet! The guests have already begun to arrive."

"I'm sorry. I was daydreaming."

"Do you need help with anything?"

"No. My costume's a little elaborate, but I can reach everything I need to."

"Have you got a wig?"

"No."

"Oh, dear. I hope your mother doesn't recognize that hair of yours."

"I'll stay on the other side of the room."

"Way on the other side of the room."

"Against the wall."

Sara grinned at her. "That'll be the day. Well, I'd better go back to my own room to see how Louis is doing."

"Louis?"

"What's Marie without her Louis? And don't laugh when you see Brian. He feels silly enough as it is."

"How does he look?"

"The way he feels." She shook her head. "I don't know how men back in those days could wear those powdered wigs and keep straight faces."

"You actually got him into a powdered wig?" Juliana asked in amazement.

"I did. And if we ever have to do something like this again, I'm going to demand combat pay."

"Well, if it's any consolation, tell Brian that he isn't going to look any sillier than anyone else."

"That's exactly what I said, but he didn't buy a word of it." She kissed Juliana's cheek. "Get yourself dressed. There's no time to lose."

"I will."

As soon as Juliana had closed her door, she went to her closet and pulled out the huge box she'd brought all the way to France with her. Inside was a silk dress that was nearly the same color as her hair. After showering, she slipped into it. The bodice was tight fitting and molded itself smoothly over each curve, exposing the creamy, soft swell of her breasts. The skirt was made up of yards and yards of silk that swung out around her, nearly touching the ground. Matching slippers peeped out from beneath the hem. She kept her makeup light and natural, and left her hair the way it was except for a small tiara that had been placed in the box with the costume. The necklace she had some trouble fastening was made of faux diamonds encircling topaz with a pendant at the bottom just touching the valley between her breasts.

Walking to the mirror, she lifted the mask to her eyes and looked at herself. The hair gave her away instantly, but other than that, she rather liked the way she looked. The dress was absolutely beautiful.

As she came down the stairs, she stopped and looked at the people below to make sure her parents weren't among them, then slipped among the elaborately gowned guests as they made their way to the ballroom. Alain, dressed in a dark tuxedo like the ones worn nearly a hundred years earlier, saw Juliana before she saw him. To him, at that moment, not only was she the most beautiful woman in the room, she was the most beautiful woman he'd ever seen.

Juliana looked up and directly into his eyes. The hand holding her mask lowered without her realizing it. She could feel the energy field between them even from fifteen feet away. It made her skin tingle.

The woman standing next to him possessively put a hand on his arm. Juliana looked at the hand and then at the woman. It was Noelle. He'd brought Noelle. When she looked back at Alain, his eyes met hers almost defiantly.

It hurt her more than she could say, and she lowered her gaze to block out the sight.

Jacques came up behind her and touched her shoulder. "Hello, Désirée. And may I say that you most definitely are."

Juliana looked up at him and smiled. "Thank you. I needed that."

"So I gathered." He glanced around the room. "Are your parents here?"

"I haven't seen them yet, but I just got here myself." She stepped back slightly and looked him up and down. "You look incredible. How long did it take you to tie that cravat?"

"More time than I've spent in a year of tying ties. Are you sure I look all right?"

"Beau Brummell, if he knew, would be proud to have you as his representative."

"High praise, indeed, considering that the man died in a lunatic asylum."

A woman walked over to them and began speaking in a rapid spate of French. Juliana listened as courteously as she could, considering she didn't understand a word. Jacques looked utterly fascinated, as though he were hanging on every syllable. When she'd gone, Jacques rolled his eyes.

"What?" Juliana asked.

"You're lucky you don't speak French."

"Why?"

"Because you would have had to listen to that."

"What was she saying?"

"Something about some boutique she's started in Paris that is, according to her, a great and instant success. She offered me an opportunity to get in on the ground floor of this already thriving enterprise."

"And what did you say?"

"That she was talking to the wrong cousin. It's all I can do to pay my rent."

"You didn't!"

"I did. I've known that woman for years and frankly, I've never been able to abide her. Her brain usually lags about three minutes behind her mouth."

Juliana watched the woman curtsy with an attractive flair in front of a man dressed as royalty. "She seems to have lovely manners."

"Humph," he muttered, unimpressed. "I think it was Voltaire who said that to be successful in this world, it isn't enough to be stupid. One must also have manners."

Juliana laughed delightedly. "Oh, thank you, Jacques. I needed that."

"Why? Problems?"

"Just the ones I bring on myself." She looked toward the door and suddenly moved behind Jacques. "They're here."

"Your parents? Where?"

"They're talking to Alain."

Charles and Claire Sheridan were dressed as members of the royal court would have dressed two hundred years earlier. Both were tall and trim, and even from where they were standing, Jacques could see that Juliana's mother was an exceptionally beautiful woman.

"Be still my heart," he said, placing his hand on his chest. "If you're going to look like that when you're however old your mother is, I definitely want to marry you."

Juliana smiled as she looked at her mother. "She's lovely, isn't she?"

"You definitely get your looks from her. Your entire family does."

Brian and Sara came up behind Juliana. "Ten minutes and then we let Mom know why she's really here."

Juliana turned her head to say something to her brother, but the sight of him in a white, curling wig momentarily robbed her of her power of speech.

Brian's eyes narrowed. "Just one word, Juliana, one word and I'll drop you from the balcony."

"We're on the ground floor."

"I'll carry you upstairs and drop you from there."

"Headfirst?"

"Of course. There's no sense in going to all that trouble if you're not going to do it right."

Juliana sucked in her cheeks. "I promise I won't say anything. Not a single word."

"Then I will," Jacques said, his eyes sparkling with laughter. "You look ridiculous. Who talked you into that getup?"

Brian glared at Sara who innocently smiled back at him and batted her lashes.

"We'll talk later," he warned her.

The rest of the family began gathering around them, even the children, all of whom had been dressed as children from another era. Kari walked over to her aunt and slipped her small hand into hers. Juliana bent until she and Kari were eye level. Juliana lightly touched Kari's silky golden hair. "Hi, honey. How are your scrapes?"

"Better."

"Good."

Kari leaned against her and looked at all the people. They must have seemed so strange to her.

"Are you tired?" Juliana asked softly.

The little girl nodded.

"Well, as soon as we tell Grandma and Grandpa that you're here and they have a chance to hug you, you can go to bed."

Juliana straightened and found that Alain was standing next to her. His shoulder lightly brushed against hers, sending a shiver of awareness down her spine. Their eyes met.

"You look beautiful, Juliana," he said quietly.

"Thank you."

"Are you ready?"

"As ready as I'll ever be."

"And the rest of you? Is everybody here?"

All of the Sheridans nodded.

"Good." He left them to walk to the front of the ballroom. The music lowered and then stopped altogether as Alain stepped onto the dais. "Good evening to you all," he said in French. Jacques standing next to Juliana, translated his cousin's words into English for her.

"As all but one of you in this room knows, there's a very definite purpose behind this ball besides the obvious one of having a good time. Two years ago an American man and woman came to Paris to live. None of us thought too much of it at the time. One ambassador is very much like another one. Or so we thought. Charles Sheridan took us to his heart. He's helped us in situations where no one else would or could. He's put himself and his career on the line, and he's done it for France, and for the relationship our country has with his. His wife, Claire, has made her own sacrifices. Coming here meant leaving her family behind. They haven't all been together under one roof for more than two years. Until tonight."

Juliana was watching her mother's bewildered face as she listened to Alain.

"Ambassador," Alain said as he stepped aside, "I think you should take it from here."

Her father turned so that he was facing his wife. He took her hands in his and gazed into her eyes in such a way that everyone in the room could feel the love between them. "As you well know," he said in English, "we've been married thirty-five years tonight. Together, with you doing most of the work, I must admit," he said with a smile, "we've brought seven wonderful children into this world and raised them well. Each has remained uniquely his or her own person and all of them continue to bring us joy. I gave a lot of thought to this anniversary, darling. Even though you love France, I know the past two years haven't been easy for you. It's difficult being away from those you love most in the world. So, to celebrate our time together in the only way imaginable, I had a little help from some friends, our host in particular. He's opened his home to us. He's given us this ball, and he's allowed our children to gather here to share this with us." He kissed his wife's cheek. "Claire, grow old along with me! The best is yet to be. I love you more today than I did the day I married you. You're the best part of my life. Happy anniversary, darling."

Her mother was in tears, but happy—and confused. All of her children, their wives, and grandchildren stepped forward. She gasped in disbelief as she looked at them.

Juliana couldn't remember ever seeing her mother at a loss for words—until now. She stopped in front of each of her children and touched their faces in wonder.

She kissed her daughters-in-law and hugged her grand-children.

A servant arrived with a tray full of glasses filled with champagne. Everyone took one. The younger Sheri-dans raised their glasses in a silent salute to their par-ents, then they all joined in a circle, their arms around each other, for a group hug.

The music began again, and Charles and Claire Sheridan came together in the middle of the ballroom to dance a waltz. About halfway through, others began joining them, and soon the room was filled with dresses gracefully sweeping the floor as couples waltzed around the perimeter.

Juliana watched as Alain went by with Noelle in his arms. His eyes met hers, but he looked away.

It was hard. She was happy for her parents, but there was a sadness inside her that she couldn't quite shake. One minute she was full of optimism, and the next she was in the depths of despair. There didn't seem to be a middle road. Or at least if there was one, she hadn't found it yet.

Sara danced by with Brian and saw the expression on Juliana's face. It nearly broke her heart because she knew the reason behind it, but there was nothing she could do for her sister-in-law.

Kari touched her aunt's hand to get her attention. "You said I could go to bed now."

Juliana smiled down at her, taking her small hand in hers. "Yes, I did. Where are your mom and dad?"

"Dancing. I told them you were going to take me and they said it was okay."

"All right, then. Let's go, honey." She lifted her up in her arms and carried her through the ballroom and up the stairs to her room.

Kari got out her footed pajamas and Juliana helped her into them, made sure she brushed her teeth, then tucked her into bed. Kari smiled up at her, and Juliana melted. "Do you want a story?"

Kari shook her head and closed her eyes.

Very gently, Juliana sat on the edge of the bed and stroked the little girl's soft hair. "Good night, sweetheart," she said softly as she looked at the long, dark lashes that rested against her rosy cheeks.

Pam opened the door a crack and peeked inside, then walked over to the bed and looked down at her daughter with smiling eyes. "How long has she been asleep?"

"Just a few minutes. I didn't want to leave her alone."

"Poor little thing. This has been a hard trip for her." Pam touched Juliana's shoulder. "Thank you for putting her to bed. Alain is sending up a maid to stay with her until the end of the party. I'll wait here for her."

"I don't mind staying."

"You go have some fun and dance until you drop. That nice cousin of Alain's was looking for you."

"Jacques?"

"Yes, that's his name. He seems quite fond of you."

"There's a reason for that. I'm probably the only unattached female down there."

"Somehow I get the impression that his reaction toward you would be the same if there were a multitude of single women around."

Juliana smiled and got up from the bed. "How are Mom and Dad doing?"

"Dancing like newlyweds."

Juliana shook her head. "Isn't it wonderful? Did you see the look on her face?"

"Your father really did it this time. I don't think he's ever been able to surprise her before. At least not like this." Pam glanced at the clock on the bedside table. "You'd better get back before you're missed. Your parents are probably already wondering what happened to you."

Juliana smiled at the little girl so soundly asleep. "Kari happened to me." Her long skirt whispered around her as she left the room and went downstairs. But instead of going to the ballroom, she went through the living room and out onto the patio. She could still hear the music. It was another waltz. She looked at the starry sky and began swaying gently back and forth, then held out her arms to an imaginary partner and began whirling around, lost in her own little world.

A hand touched her waist and another took her hand in his. Juliana opened her eyes to find Alain gazing down at her. Without saying a word, his eyes never leaving hers, he began moving with her, guiding her around the patio with such skill that she didn't have to think about her own movement at all. The hand at her waist was warm and strong. She felt it through the silk of her dress, and there wasn't a moment when she wasn't completely aware that it was there, touching her.

The fingers of her right hand twined in his. He held her closer, yet their bodies never touched.

Juliana's eyes moved to his mouth and rested there. She remembered so vividly how it felt against hers.

The music ended. The couple stopped moving, but Alain's hand remained at her waist and their fingers were still meshed. His dark eyes moved slowly over every feature of her lovely face as though memorizing it.

Then, as silently as he'd come, he left.

It was in that moment that Juliana knew that she'd never see him again. Not if he could help it.

Juliana wrapped her arms around herself and stared at the sky as she released a trembling breath.

Chapter Seven

Juliana sat on the grassy hill, the warm Wisconsin sun highlighting her hair. A large sketch pad rested on her bare, tanned legs. The blank white page had been transformed into a skillfully executed sketch of flower beds, walkways, a natural-looking stream and small waterfall that bore little resemblance to the overgrown, weed-infested lawn that stretched in front of her. By this time next year, though, the lawn would look like the drawing.

The movement of the pencil slowed and then stopped altogether as Juliana stared absently into the distance, not really seeing what was there. Her mind wasn't on her work. It had been three months since she'd left France, but part of her had stayed behind.

"Hey, Juliana!"

She turned her head to find her business partner running across the lawn toward her. A welcoming smile curved her mouth. "Ben, what are you doing here?"

He collapsed onto the ground next to her, panting, his hand over his heart. "Good grief," he gasped. "I can't believe there are actually people in this world who run for pleasure."

A dimple creased Juliana's cheek as she smiled at him. "Face it, Benjamin, you're out of shape," she said affectionately as she went back to work.

"I'm in terrific shape."

"For a man of sixty," she said dryly. "Which would be great if you weren't only twenty-five."

"Twenty-six."

"Oh, well, that explains it. The difference between twenty-five and twenty-six can be a killer."

Ben grinned at her as he lay back on the grass. His gaze moved to the blue sky with soft white clouds. "Mmmmmm," he sighed happily. "What a beautiful fall day this has been."

"Umm-hmm," Juliana agreed absently as she put the finishing touches on her work and studied it critically. "What do you think?"

"About what?"

"My design for this area of the yard."

"I can't see it."

Juliana held the pad in front of him, blocking the sky. Ben's expert eye moved over every inch of the drawing. "Well?" she asked anxiously after a moment.

He took the pad from her and held it high in the air. "I like it, Juliana. For the most part."

"For the most part? What does that mean?"

"Exactly what you think it means."

"What's wrong with it?"

"To tell you the truth, I like it the way it is, but I think you're going to run into problems with the clients over what you've done to the left of the stream."

"You mean the more formal garden?"

Ben nodded. "You heard what they said about wanting everything to look as natural as possible. That garden looks designed."

"I did that on purpose. If you follow the path," she said as she touched the pad with her long, tapered finger, "you can see that I've done exactly what the clients want. Everything looks as though nature did it. But this garden I've planned is almost like an oasis. Imagine what a delightful surprise a person walking along that path will have when he suddenly finds himself in the middle of a riot of color."

"I know what you're doing. As I said, I like it. But you're not designing it for me."

Juliana sighed. "I suppose I could toss a few weeds among the flowers, just for effect."

Ben laughed and handed her back the pad.

She laid it across her lap and tapped a pencil on the drawing as she looked it over again. "I did it the other way in my first sketch. I think what I'll do is show them both ideas and let them choose—with a little biased guidance from the designer."

"That's the best way. When do you have your next meeting with them?"

"Monday." Juliana flipped the cover over the drawing and began packing up her pencils. "I'm going to head home. Are you and Penny doing anything exciting this weekend?"

"We're going out to dinner. It's our anniversary."

Juliana glanced sideways at him. "Anniversary? This is September. You were married in November."

"Ah, but we met in September. Two years ago tonight at 7:15, to be precise."

Juliana zipped her large purse closed and sat back on her heels. "That's nice that you remember something like that."

"Nice? Try self-preservation. I forgot about that fateful day last year and Penny didn't talk to me for a month."

"Serves you right."

"You women always stick together."

Juliana grinned at him. The two of them had known each other since grade school. He was as much a brother to her as her real ones. "Stop trying to pretend you're like most other men. You're not, you know."

"That's just between us, all right?"

"I haven't told anyone yet, have I?"

"True."

Juliana sighed as she gazed into the distance.

Ben raised his hand to shield his eyes from the sun as he turned his head to look up at her profile. He was silent for a long time, just watching her.

Juliana turned her head and looked down at him. "You're staring at me."

"I know. What's wrong?"

"What makes you think something's wrong?"

"Eighteen years of friendship."

Juliana shook her head. "Sometimes I think you know me a little too well. Something has been bothering me, but talking about it with you or anyone else isn't going to help."

"You could try," he suggested.

"No. Thanks anyway."

"All right. I guess a change of subject is in order. You know what my plans are for the night. What are yours?"

Juliana lifted her shoulders. "I don't really know. Run on the beach and perhaps go to a movie."

"With anyone I know?"

"Just me." She looked at him threateningly. "And don't you dare tell Penny. I know she means well, but if she tries to set me up with one more blind date, I'm leaving town. Her taste in men leaves a lot to be desired."

Ben lifted an expressive brow.

"Present company excluded, of course."

"That's better. And don't worry. Your secret's safe with me. To tell you the truth, though, I don't think it's Penny's taste in men that's the problem."

Juliana sighed. "Here it comes."

"Here what comes?"

"The lecture."

"I never lecture you." He paused for a moment. "I simply tell you when you're doing something wrong."

"And what, exactly, am I doing wrong?"

Ben grew serious. "You're waiting for Prince Charming," he said quietly, "and he's not out there."

Juliana's smile was soft as she shook her head. "Oh, yes, he is. Well, actually, he's a Duc, and there are times when he's not very charming, but he's there. He's just not coming for me."

A frown creased Ben's forehead. "What are you talking about? Does this have something to do with France?"

"Leave France out of this."

Ben swore suddenly and sat up.

Juliana looked at him in surprise. "What's wrong?"

"I had a reason for coming out here other than admiring the scenery. Your dad called the office and told me to have you call him back as soon as you could."

"Is something wrong?"

"He didn't say, but he didn't sound upset or anything."

"I'd better go." She got to her feet, shouldered her bag and tucked the drawing pad under her arm. "You have a nice night. Give Penny my love."

"I will. Talk to you tomorrow."

Juliana crossed the yard to where her yellow Jeep was parked, put everything onto the passenger seat and headed home.

Alain paced back and forth in the American ambassador's office. Walking behind the desk, he looked out the window onto the Paris street and watched the cars for a few minutes, then turned. A picture on the desk caught his eye. It was of the Sheridan family. Juliana's smiling face was in the middle of all of her brothers. He picked up the picture and held it in both hands as he looked at her. Not a day had gone by since she'd left that he hadn't thought about her. His thumb lightly traced her cheek. The muscle in his jaw tightened.

Charles Sheridan walked in and smiled at the man behind his desk. "Alain, thanks for coming so quickly."

Alain put the picture back on the desk and gave his attention to the ambassador. "It sounded important on the phone."

"It is." The two men changed places, with the ambassador going behind his desk and Alain taking a chair in front of it. The older man searched through some papers until he found what he was looking for and pushed it across to the Frenchman. "Read this and tell me what you think."

Alain quickly scanned the letter, then he went over it again more carefully. "I don't understand what it is that you want me to do."

"You have far-reaching contacts in the international banking world. I need to know anything you can get me on this man."

"Why?"

"He's interfering in some sensitive negotiations we've undertaken between France and the U.S. Before I confront him, I want to know what kind of money he has behind him and who's supplying him with it."

"Can I keep this?" Alain asked, indicating the letter.

"Of course."

He folded it and put it into his pocket. "I'll check and get back to you."

"Be discreet."

"I always am."

Charles Sheridan leaned back in his chair and studied the Frenchman. He had a very real fondness for him. "Are you free for lunch today?"

"I'm afraid not."

"You haven't been free for lunch for several months. Not since my family stayed at your château. Does one have something to do with the other?"

"Not at all."

A secretary opened the door and looked in. "Ambassador, your daughter is on line one, returning your call."

Alain started to rise, but the older man waved him back in his seat. "I won't be a minute. Juliana!" he said with a smile as he pushed the speaker button.

Alain reluctantly lowered himself back into the chair. A moment later, Juliana's lovely voice filled the room. "Hello, Dad. Ben told me you called the office. Is everything all right?"

"Everything's fine. I've got you on the speaker. Say hello to Alain. He's here with me."

Juliana clutched her receiver with both hands. Several seconds went by.

"J. J., are you still there?"

"I'm here, Dad. Hello, Alain."

"Hello," the Frenchman said quietly.

"Honey, your mom is going to be coming to the U.S. in a few weeks to have some minor surgery that she's been putting off."

"Surgery? What's wrong?"

"Nothing that's life threatening, believe me. She's going to be in New York near Brian and Sara and they've agreed to watch over her while she's there. The problem is that I need someone here during the time she'll be gone to help with some social functions."

"Oh, Dad, I don't know. I'm very busy right now."

"I know, but I wouldn't ask if it weren't important. And it would put your mother's mind at ease to know that things here were taken care of."

Her parents so rarely asked anything of her. Despite what she was feeling, she couldn't say no. "Of course, Dad. When do you want me there?"

"Is three weeks too soon?"

"No. I'll be there." She paused again. "Goodbye, Alain."

"Juliana."

"See you soon, Dad."

When she'd hung up the phone, Juliana sat with her hand on the receiver for a long time. It gave her a strange feeling to know exactly where Alain was at that moment. She turned her head and gazed out at the lake. She felt an unutterable sadness.

Charles Sheridan flipped the switch that cut off the call and pursed his lips. "I wish I knew what was bothering her," he said more to himself than to the man with him.

"What do you mean?"

"She's unhappy about something. I can hear it in her voice. But she won't talk to anyone about it."

"Perhaps you're imagining it."

He shook his head. "No. Juliana is one of the most naturally optimistic people I know. You must have noticed that when she was staying with you."

Alain was silent.

"Something has happened to shake it." He looked at the Frenchman. "Maybe coming to Paris will help."

Alain looked at his watch. It was impossible to tell what he was thinking. "I have to be going." He rose and held out his hand. "As always, Ambassador, it's been a pleasure."

Charles rose also.

"I'll be in touch soon," Alain said and left the embassy.

As soon as he got back to his office, he sat behind his desk and buzzed his secretary. When she came in a moment later, he didn't even look up. "I want you to make arrangements for me to visit my other banks beginning in three weeks."

"In three weeks? But you have those men coming in from Saudi Arabia."

"Change it. I don't want to be in France."

"But..."

He looked up and his dark eyes nailed her to the wall. "Miss Giscard..."

Her shoulders straightened. "Yes, sir."

As soon as she'd gone, Alain spun around in his chair and stared out the window. He was angry. Angry with Juliana for coming back to France and angry with himself for caring one way or another.

A week later, Juliana stood in her room at the ambassador's residence looking at herself in the mirror. The bodice of the off-the-shoulder black dress fit snugly to just below her hips, then flared out to the middle of her knees. A delicate single-strand diamond bracelet circled her wrist. She finished fastening the diamond earrings and made one more pass at her curls with a brush, then went downstairs where her father was waiting in the hallway dressed in his tuxedo.

He gave a low whistle when he saw her. "What are the chances that I'm going to be coming home with my date tonight?" he asked with a smile.

"Better than even."

He wrapped a black cape around her shoulders. "You know, if you meet a young man there and he happens to invite you out for a cognac and coffee, I won't be offended."

"I'm old-fashioned, Dad. I like the same date who picks me up to bring me home."

"Ordinarily I'd say bravo—or would that be *brava*? Whatever. But in this instance, your date is your father, and you're in Paris. Enjoy."

Juliana looked at him curiously as he held open the door for her. "Is that why you asked me to come two weeks early? Are you trying to find me a man?"

"I would never interfere in your life in such an obvious way."

"Of course you would."

Charles Sheridan grinned at his daughter. "All right. I would. But as it happens, I'm innocent this time. As I told you, your mother quite on her own decided to leave here ahead of schedule. She's been a little anxious ever since she found out Sara's pregnant. Even though Sara and Brian both keep telling her that everything is fine, your mother isn't going to believe it until she sees for herself."

"I just talked to Sara last night. She really is all right."

"Oh, your mother's a worrier."

"And you're not?"

"Not as much."

There was a warm smile behind Juliana's eyes as she looked at her father. "Baloney."

"J.J., you wound me. My children are all adults with their own lives to lead. I'm not a bit worried about any of you. Especially you."

Juliana lifted a brow expressively.

Her father tried to look offended. "Have I ever lied to you?"

"Only when it was for the greater good. I'm just wondering what you think the greater good is in this instance."

The chauffeur had opened the door of the long limousine and the ambassador and his daughter climbed inside. As soon as the car was moving, he touched Juliana's arm. "Sweetheart, I know something's been bothering you. I'll admit that I've been concerned about you since that week we spent at the Château de Lumiere. So has your mother. Something happened there to change you.''

''Maybe I grew up a little.''

''Maybe.''

Juliana stared out the window as the limousine moved through the lovely Paris streets.

''Is there something going on between you and Alain de Bournier?''

Juliana turned her head sharply. ''Why do you ask that?''

''Because I've thought and thought about what could have happened and always I come back to him. Nothing else makes any sense.''

Juliana looked out the window again. ''There's nothing going on between the Duc and myself.''

''By whose choice?''

Juliana was silent for a moment. ''His.''

''I see.'' His hand covered hers. ''I'm sorry.''

Juliana looked at her father and smiled. ''It's all right, really. I'm fine.''

The chauffeur parked in front of a brightly lit home and opened the doors for them. Juliana looped her arm through her father's as they climbed the stairs to the door. A uniformed servant greeted them politely and took Juliana's wrap. Another servant led them through the foyer into a salon where perhaps twenty people were gathered having drinks and conversation. Her father introduced her to the first couple they met. They were from Spain. A man who joined them was from Sweden. Everyone was speaking English since it was a language common to all of them.

Juliana, a glass of wine in her hand, laughed at something one of the men said and looked up to find Alain watching her from across the room. She had no idea how long she stood staring at him, but it must have been quite some time. Her father lightly touched her arm to bring her back to her surroundings. He'd seen Alain as well.

"Would you like to leave?" he asked her quietly.

"No, of course not." She kissed his cheek. "But thank you for asking."

"If you change your mind, just tell me."

"I will."

Alain made his way across the room to them. He shook hands with her father and then turned his attention to Juliana. "I understood that you weren't going to be here for two more weeks."

"Plans changed."

His gaze moved over her face. "You're looking well."

"So are you," she said quietly.

He gazed at her for a moment longer, inclined his head toward her father and turned away.

It seemed forever before dinner was served. Juliana, much to her dismay, found herself seated directly across the table from Alain.

She tried so hard not to look at him, but she couldn't help herself. She was hungry for the sight of him.

Alain, for his part, acknowledged that she was there, but nothing more. He spoke to the man on his left and the woman on his right. Juliana spoke to her dinner partners as well, but every time Alain looked at her, she could feel it. She wondered if he could feel her eyes on him, too.

The dinner, which was intended to introduce some of the newer diplomats to the older ones, and all of them to a few of the more important businessmen in Paris, seemed to go on forever. Course after course was served. Wine after wine. Many of the guests smoked between courses and the dining room grew warm and stuffy. Juliana drank a bit more wine than she was used to.

When it was finally over, all Juliana wanted to do was go outside into the fresh air. Her father followed her and draped her cape around her shoulders. "Rather dull, I'm afraid," he said by way of apology, "but necessary."

"I didn't mind."

"Do you think you can stand another few weeks of this?"

She smiled up at him. "Dad, I said that I didn't mind."

He opened the door of their car for her. She slid across the seat and he climbed in next to her. "I'm going home because I have an early appointment tomorrow, but if you have someplace you'd like to go, the driver will take you."

Alain came out of the house at that moment. His eyes met hers.

Juliana settled back in her seat. "I'm with you."

It didn't take long to get home. Juliana went straight to her room and got ready for bed. Lying there, she tried to read but couldn't concentrate. Putting her book on the bedside table, she got up and began pacing. She literally bubbled inside with emotion. There were so many things she needed to say and there was only one man she needed to say them to.

Picking up the phone next to her bed, Juliana pressed the chauffeur's extension.

His sleepy voice answered a moment later.

"Hi. This is Juliana. I'm sorry to bother you at this hour, but there's someplace I need to go."

The man cleared his throat. "All right. I'll meet you in front in ten minutes."

"Thank you."

Juliana dressed quickly in slim-fitting jeans and a sweater and went downstairs. By the time she walked out the front door, the driver was there holding the rear door open for her. "Do you know where the Château de Lumiere is?" she asked as she slipped into the backseat.

"Yes. I've often taken your father there."

"That's where I'd like to go."

In silence, he drove her out of Paris and into the country. Juliana's fingers drummed on the upholstery until the car pulled onto the tree-lined driveway. Then she grew completely still except for the beating of her heart.

She was almost relieved when she saw that there were lights on inside the château. Not that it would have made any difference. What she had to say wasn't going to wait.

As soon as the car had stopped, she jumped out and banged the knocker on the door. Several minutes passed before Marcel appeared. "Miss Sheridan," he said in surprise. "I'm afraid you aren't expected."

"I know. Please tell Alain that I'm here."

"He went out riding."

She knew exactly where he'd gone. "Marcel, may I borrow a horse?"

"Yes, of course."

"Thank you." She started to walk away, but turned back. "It's nice to see you again."

The butler smiled at her. "You've been missed, Miss Sheridan."

"Wait for me here," she told her driver as she ran around the house and to the stables hidden from view. There were several horses in stalls. She picked one at random and climbed onto his back without a saddle.

It was exhilarating feeling the power of the horse beneath her and the crisp wind as it hit her face. Far from calming her down, it stirred her up even more.

She found Alain on the hill, sitting on the grass while his horse grazed nearby. He rose as soon as he saw her. "What are you doing here?" he asked as she climbed down from the horse.

"I came to talk to you."

"There's nothing to talk about."

"Maybe not for you, but I have some things to say. Things I should have said months ago but didn't."

"This is hardly the time for this."

She walked toward him, her eyes meeting his in the moonlight. "I'm only going to be in France a short time," she said quietly, "and my guess is that you're going to do your best to avoid me, so now is as good a time as any."

Alain just stood there.

"You know, when I was in my room tonight, I knew exactly what I wanted to say, and now that I'm here, I don't seem to be nearly as articulate." She took a deep breath and forced herself to meet his eyes with a direct gaze of her own.

"When I came here in June, something happened to me that I never expected. I fell in love with you. I think I knew at the time that it was hopeless, but I couldn't talk myself out of it. And I'll tell you something else, Alain. I think you fell in love with me as well."

Alain continued looking at her, but said nothing.

"You pushed me away and I let you because I didn't know what else to do. And you pushed me away because you didn't know what else to do. To do otherwise would have meant that you'd have to confront your own feelings, and I don't think you've ever done that before. You think you're a man who can go through life on the surface without anything ever really touching you. The minute you grow uncomfortable with feelings, you eliminate them from your life, just the way you eliminated me from your life. You crave the safety of numbness. You thrive on it."

A muscle in Alain's jaw clenched.

"I can't make you deal with your feelings. I can only try to deal with my own. But I can tell you that you're throwing away a chance for happiness. Yours and mine."

Juliana climbed onto the horse and started to leave, but turned back to him. Her eyes moved over his face. "God, I wish I could make you see what a terrible mistake you're making in turning away from me. I wish I could make you understand how wonderful it is to feel deeply about people. There's pain, yes, but there are such rewards as well." Her throat tightened and tears filled her eyes. "I love you so much."

After looking at him for a long, quiet moment, she turned the horse and rode off.

Alain stood unmoving, staring into the night. Juliana's words echoed in his mind. So much of what she'd said was right. He did like being numb. He liked living in a world where nothing was really that important to him. Where people passed through his life, but never really left a mark.

At least that's the way it had been until Juliana Sheridan. She said that he was in love with her. Was he? He desired her. That was a kind of love, but certainly not what she was talking about. She did make him feel things, and he'd pushed those feelings aside rather than pursuing them.

Alain dragged his fingers through his hair. Why couldn't she have simply stayed in America? Everything would have been fine.

Juliana sat in silence on the drive home. The chauffeur kept glancing at her in the rearview mirror to make sure she was all right. He had no idea what had gone on but it obviously hadn't been very pleasant for her.

When he parked in front of the ambassador's residence, Juliana climbed out of the car and looked up at the driver. "Thank you for taking me."

"Of course."

Her father opened the door, sending a shaft of light shining onto the driveway.

Juliana smiled tiredly as she walked toward him. The ambassador put his arm around her shoulders and walked her inside, closing the door behind them. "Did you go to see Alain?"

She nodded.

"What happened?"

"I just said what I had to and left."

"What did he say?"

"Not a word. Not a single word."

Her father put his hands on her shoulders and quoted softly, "One broken dream is not the end of dreaming; One shattered hope is not the end of all—Beyond the storm and tempests stars are gleaming—Still build your castles, though your castles fall."

Juliana rose on her toes and kissed his cheek. "Thanks, Dad."

"Are you going to be all right?"

She nodded.

"Do you want me to send up some warm milk?"

A heartbreaking smile touched her mouth. "Why couldn't I have fallen in love with someone as nice as you?"

He touched his hand to her silky hair. "Maybe you will yet. You're still young."

"At the moment, I feel very old."

He kissed the top of her head. "I know. I wish there was something I could do, but I know I can't."

"No, you can't," she said quietly. "Good night, Dad."

"Good night, sweetheart."

Chapter Eight

Juliana looked at her watch as she waited for the chauffeur to pick them up. Six more hours and she'd be on the plane home.

Her father smiled as he noticed what she was doing. "Counting the minutes?"

"The hours. I've enjoyed spending this time with you, but it's going to be nice to go home and get back to work."

"Have you talked to Ben lately?"

"Just last night."

"Is everything all right?"

"Busy. The landscaping season is winding down, but there's still new construction going on and people want their lawns designed and ready for spring."

"Well, by this time tomorrow you'll be able to call your life your own once again. There's the car." He put his hand under her arm and walked her down the steps of the hotel where they'd been having lunch.

The sidewalk was fairly crowded as they stepped into the mainstream of pedestrian traffic and tried to cross it to get to their car.

Suddenly someone shouted and shoved Juliana from behind, sending her crashing to the pavement. Shots rang out and the people around her screamed and ran. She knew instantly what was happening. "Dad!" she screamed as she scrambled to her feet. "Dad!" She saw him being rushed unceremoniously toward the street.

The years of touch football with her brothers paid off as she darted and dodged through the people on the sidewalk and literally hurled herself at the back of the man who had her father. She clung to him as tenaciously as a puppy. He tried to shake her off, but she wouldn't let go. All she knew was that if she did, she'd never see her father again.

The man dragged her, kicking and screaming for help, all the way to a car. Another man who was in the car pulled her struggling father inside, then shouted at the man Juliana was clinging to, in a language she didn't understand. Free of her father, it was easier for him to maneuver. He flipped her over in front of him and crooked his arm around her neck. She bit him, and he let go with a shout, raised his hand and hit her hard, sending her flying against the car. She heard another shot and felt a searing pain in her shoulder.

That was the last thing she remembered.

* * *

That evening, Alain was in his hotel room in Rome getting ready to go out to dinner. He turned on a radio and went into the bathroom to shave. He heard nothing while the water was running, but as soon as he turned the faucet off, he heard something about the American ambassador to France.

Walking quickly back into the room, his heart filled with a sudden foreboding, he sat on the edge of the bed and changed stations, listening for another news broadcast. He couldn't find one. Swearing softly under his breath, he picked up the phone and dialed his office number.

As soon as his secretary answered, he cut her off. "Miss Giscard. What's the news about the American ambassador?"

"It happened this afternoon."

"What happened?"

"He was abducted at gunpoint outside a hotel."

Alain closed his eyes and gave himself a moment of silence before asking the next question. "Was his daughter with him?"

"Yes. They apparently took her as well. Some witnesses said she was shot."

"Oh, my God," he said softly, and then was silent.

"Sir?" his secretary said after a few uneasy moments. "Are you still on the line?"

"Yes. I'm coming home right away. I want you to call Ambassador Sheridan's wife and tell her that I'll be coming straight to her home from the airport."

"But she's been out of the country. At least that's what the news has been saying."

"You can bet she was on her way back within minutes after she heard the news."

"Is there anything else I can do?"

"Just cancel everything on my calendar for an indefinite period of time."

"Yes, sir."

He hung up and quickly finished getting dressed. Leaving everything behind but his briefcase, he went to the airport, and caught a flight to Paris.

In reality, it was a short flight, but to Alain it seemed to take forever. As soon as his plane landed, he rushed through customs and then through the airport to a taxi stand. It was faster than waiting for his driver.

Sitting in the backseat of the cab, his dark eyes stared unseeingly out the window. If anything had happened to Juliana...

He leaned forward to address the driver. "Faster."

When they finally arrived at the ambassador's house, there was no place to park. The street was lined with cars and government employees milled around outside. The driver let him out near the front door.

A large man, obviously a security guard, put his hand on Alain's shoulder to stop him from entering the house. Alain looked from the man to the man's hand and back to the man.

The security guard's hand fell to his side. "This is a restricted area. You'll have to leave."

"Mrs. Sheridan is expecting me."

"And you are?"

"Alain de Bournier."

"Just a minute." The guard entered the house and returned a few minutes later. "All right. You may pass."

Claire Sheridan entered the foyer at the same time as Alain. She was pale and frightened looking. "You heard what happened?" she asked.

"Yes."

She shook her head. "Someone just took them. They put guns in their backs and took them away." Her eyes filled with tears. "I wish I knew what to do."

Alain wanted to offer her comfort, but he didn't know how. How could you comfort someone who had lost so much so quickly? "Do you know who the kidnappers are?"

"No. So far I've been told nothing except that the kidnappers have been in contact."

"Did they say anything about Juliana?"

"No, not specifically."

"What about a ransom? Has one been demanded?"

"I'm told that one has been, but they wouldn't tell me how much."

"What is your government doing about getting Juliana and your husband back?"

"There's nothing they can do. It's their policy to pay nothing to kidnappers for fear that it would only encourage others to do the same thing."

It made good sense, but they weren't just talking in vague terms. This was Juliana and the ambassador. He couldn't leave it at that. "Who's in charge of the case?"

"A man came here with me from the State Department. His name is Carl Briscoe."

"Where is he now?"

"At the embassy."

"I'm going to go see him."

"They'll never let you in."

"Then you come with me."

She looked at him for a long moment. She'd known Alain for two years. He'd always been very polite to her. It was clear that he thought highly of her husband— perhaps even had some affection for him. But she'd always been aware that there were certain boundaries one didn't cross with Alain. He wasn't someone she would ever consider treating with familiarity. Frankly, he wasn't someone she would have expected to help her husband with getting their children in one place for their anniversary. And at the moment she wasn't quite sure why he was getting involved now. All she knew was that she needed all the help she could get, and if he was willing to offer it, she wasn't about to turn him down. "All right. Let me get my coat."

Alain paced the hallway until she returned, then walked her outside and hailed a taxi. Within minutes, they were at the embassy. The guards tried to stop Alain from entering, but Claire insisted and the two of them were allowed to pass. They walked straight through to the ambassador's office. A nondescript man somewhere in his early forties rose from behind the desk. "Mrs. Sheridan, I wish I had some news for you, but I don't."

"Have you heard anything at all from the kidnappers?" Alain asked.

The man looked at him. "Who are you?"

"Alain de Bournier."

"What do you have to do with any of this?"

"I'm a—friend of the family. And you are?"

"Carl Briscoe. I'm with the State Department."

"What are you doing about securing their release?"

"I'm not at liberty to discuss—"

"I understand that a ransom has been demanded."

The man from the State Department looked at Claire Sheridan. "How much have you told him?"

"Everything that you told me."

Mr. Briscoe returned to his seat. "Then it would appear that you know everything that we know."

It took Alain a moment to ask the next question. "Are they still alive?"

"Probably. We have no way of being sure, of course. It's believed that the girl was shot. She might well be dead."

Claire Sheridan, even though she'd heard of the shooting already, gasped at the harshness of the words.

"The girl's name is Juliana," Alain said tersely.

The American looked at him in surprise. "I'm sorry. Juliana is believed to have been unconscious when she was put in the car."

Alain was silent. His mouth tightened. His already dark eyes grew darker. It was then that Claire Sheridan knew why Alain was there.

"Do you know who the people are who took them?" Alain asked.

"Yes."

"Well?" he probed impatiently when no further information was forthcoming.

"You must understand, Mr. de Bournier, I can't discuss this with you."

"Mr. Briscoe," Juliana's mother said firmly, "You can trust this man. My husband does. I would think at this point that you'd want all the help you can get. Perhaps the Duc can help."

The man thought about it for a moment, then rose. "Excuse me. I'll be right back."

Neither Alain nor the ambassador's wife said anything while they waited, each lost in their own thoughts. The man returned after about fifteen minutes. "Mrs. Sheridan, will you excuse us for a short while?"

She started to protest, but Alain touched her arm. "It's all right."

She looked into his eyes and knew quite clearly in that moment that this was a man she could trust with the lives of her husband and daughter. Inclining her head, and without saying another word, she left the two men alone.

Alain turned to the American as soon as she had gone. "All right. Tell me what you know."

Carl Briscoe waved the Frenchman into the chair across from him. "I have to warn you ahead of time that it isn't much. The group who grabbed the ambassador and his daughter is called the Middle East Freedom Fighters. Until today, they'd limited themselves to snatching diplomats and university professors off their own streets. Now, however, it would appear that they've decided to branch out.''

''How have they treated their other hostages?''

''Not well. They killed three of their hostages when deadlines they'd set weren't met by countries that refused to be blackmailed. A few others were released after only the briefest of captivities when ransoms were paid. Others have remained in captivity for over two years. What their condition is is anyone's guess.''

''Do you have any idea where Juliana and her father are being held?''

''None. To be honest, we don't even know if they're still in France.''

Alain shook his head. ''You don't know much of anything, do you?''

''What can I tell you, Mr. de Bournier? They caught us by surprise.''

Alain grew thoughtful. ''Tell me this, then. Since you know they want a ransom, you've obviously had some contact with the kidnappers. What kind of negotiations are you currently involved in?''

''None.''

Alain looked at him in disbelief. ''None? What do you mean, none?''

''I mean that it's the policy of the government of the United States not to pay terrorists for the release of hostages.''

''I understand that, but what happens to the hostages?''

''Don't misunderstand me, Mr. de Bournier. We do talk with the groups who take hostages and we'll talk with this group. But if we begin paying these people for the release of our citizens, no one will be safe. Every time some terrorist needs money, and they always need money, he'll grab a citizen.''

"So if you don't pay them, what exactly is it that you talk to them about?''

"We explain our policy, and we explain what the repercussions will be if any harm comes to an American while that American is in their custody.''

"And what are those repercussions?''

"Honestly? Unless we find the terrorists, and that's at best an iffy proposition, nothing.''

"And if you do find them?''

"Imprisonment. Possible backlash against their families and their organization.''

A corner of Alain's mouth lifted. "And this is supposed to frighten them into releasing the hostages?''

"It's all we can do.''

Alain shook his head, rose from his chair and walked over to the window. "What kind of ransom is being demanded?''

"Two hundred million dollars.''

He swore under his breath and turned to the American. "How do they expect anyone to come up with that kind of money?''

"As far as the MEFF is concerned, they have an American ambassador. The American government is a bottomless well of revenue. They think that despite our telling them that we won't pay, we'll change our minds.''

Alain looked out the window again. For a long time he said nothing. "What if you were to find someone willing to supply the ransom?"

"You can't be serious."

His dark eyes zeroed in on the American. "I said, what if you were to find someone willing to supply the ransom?"

"It wouldn't make any difference. Our policy is not to pay kidnappers."

"All right. That's your policy. Now let me tell you about my policy. I'm going to get that money and if I have to negotiate with the terrorists myself to get the ambassador and Juliana back, that's what I'm going to do. If you choose to cooperate with me, that would be even better, but regardless of your decision, it won't change my actions."

The American eyed the man. "You can come up with that kind of money?"

"It won't be easy, but yes, I can."

"And how do you plan on getting in touch with these people?"

"I'll find a way."

The American believed him. "Do you understand that the chances of your getting your money back are very slim?"

"The money isn't the issue."

"Don't kid yourself, de Bournier. The money *is* the issue, and as far as the kidnappers are concerned, it's the only issue. They couldn't care less about Charles and Juliana Sheridan."

Alain's dark eyes bored into the other man. "Are you going to help me or not?"

There was silence in the room for a long time. "You understand," the American said quietly, "that any assistance we give you will be strictly unofficial, and that whatever happens we'll deny any involvement."

"I understand."

"Good."

"It's my opinion that the kidnappers don't really need Juliana. In fact, if she's hurt and there's a chance that she could die in their custody, it could become a liability."

"That's true. So?"

"So I want it suggested to the kidnappers that no negotiations will be considered until Juliana is released alive. And in the meantime, I want proof that she's alive."

"What makes you think they'll go along with this?"

"Because they want the money."

"I hope you're right. I'll do what I can." The American rose and extended his hand. "I'll get back to you."

Alain extended his hand as well.

He found Mrs. Sheridan in one of the meeting rooms. She rose from the couch as soon as she saw him. "Well?"

"I can't give you any details, but certain things are being worked out."

"Are they going to be all right, Alain?" Her fingers dug painfully into his forearm.

He looked steadily into her eyes—eyes so much like Juliana's. "Yes. I won't have it any other way." He looked around the empty room. "You shouldn't be alone at a time like this."

"I won't be for long. My family is coming. In fact, Brian should be here soon."

"Would you like me to stay here with you until he arrives?"

She shook her head. "I'll be all right."

"I wouldn't ordinarily leave you, but there are things I must take care of right away."

"I understand, really." Her eyes suddenly filled with tears. "What am I saying? I don't understand at all. Not any of this. Why would they take Charles? He's such a good man. He's never hurt anyone in his life." She shook her head. "And Juliana. In a few hours she would have been on her way back to America. She's just the ambassador's daughter. What could they possibly want with her?"

Alain, uneasy with a woman's tears, put his hand on her shoulder and squeezed. "They'll come back to you."

She put her hand over his. "Thank you for coming, Alain. I know it would mean a lot to Juliana if she knew."

Alain's eyes met hers, then he turned and left the embassy to go to his office. Jacques was already there and sprang to his feet as soon as his cousin entered.

"Did you hear about Juliana and her father?"

Alain closed the door behind him. "I just came from the embassy."

"What have they heard? Are they all right?"

Alain sat behind his desk and dragged his fingers tiredly through his hair. "No one knows." He looked at his cousin. "Jacques, I need your help."

"With what?"

"I have to raise a lot of money very quickly."

"For what?"

"A ransom."

"But why you?"

"Because I'm the only one who can. Don't ask any more questions; just do as I ask. Please."

Jacques sat down again, watching his cousin with a curious look. "All right." He'd never seen Alain like this.

"I want you to go through my stocks and sell them for the best price you can get."

Jacques blinked. "All of them?"

"All of them. And while you're doing that, I have to try to find a buyer for the château."

Jacques was shocked and it showed. "A buyer for the château? You can't be serious."

Alain looked straight at his cousin. "I've never been more serious in my life. Have my secretary give you my stock portfolio and show you to an empty office."

Jacques rose, but still looked at his cousin. "Who are you going to sell it to?"

"There's an American who's been after it for years. Another notch on his belt of ownership."

Jacques knew exactly who Alain was talking about, and he also knew the kind of contempt his cousin held that particular American in. Without making any comment, Jacques turned and left the office.

Alain sat deep in thought. There were banks he could sell off, but selling businesses, between finding buyers and government red tape, could take months. He didn't have the luxury of that kind of time.

Juliana lay in the silence, aware. She slowly opened her eyes, but it didn't help. The room was dark. Her shoulder felt as though it were on fire. Where was she? The last thing she remembered was having lunch with her father, and then there were those men and the shots.

There was a commotion outside the room. The door was suddenly opened, flooding the room with a light that blinded her. Something was shoved inside, then the door was slammed shut and everything was black again.

She could hear something alive in the room. "Who's here? Is anyone here?"

"Juliana?"

"Dad!"

He made his way across the room to her, feeling his way along the wall. "Are you all right?"

"No."

He found her lying on a cot and touched his fingers to her face. His heart sank. She was so hot.

"Is there any water, Dad? I'm thirsty."

The ambassador went to the door and banged his fist on it. "My daughter is ill. She needs a doctor. Please. Is anyone out there?"

There was no answer.

"Can we at least have some water?"

His only answer was silence. He made his way back to Juliana. "I'm sorry."

"It's all right. They'll probably come back soon."

He stroked her hair away from her dry face as he sat on the floor beside her, feeling helpless in the way only a parent can. "This is all my fault," he said in a choked voice. "I should have let you stay in Wisconsin instead of dragging you back to France."

"I wanted to come. And the situation we're in is hardly your fault, Dad. It's not anybody's fault except the people who took us." She tried to sit up, but the pain was so excruciating that she nearly passed out.

"Juliana? Juliana?" Her father's tone was panicked.

"I'm all right." Her voice was too hoarse to be convincing. "Do you know who they are?"

"The kidnappers? No. They've only spoken to me to give me orders. Frankly it doesn't really matter who they are. If they're terrorists, and I think they are, their usual pattern is for them to blackmail governments for money while promising to release the hostages unharmed."

Juliana was flooded with relief. "That's not so bad, then. All we have to do is wait for our government to pay them off and we can go home."

The ambassador brushed his mouth against her hair and didn't tell her what he knew.

"How long do you think it'll take?"

"I don't know, Juliana. I just don't know."

The small room grew silent.

Chapter Nine

Alain was back at the embassy within seventy-two hours looking much the worse for wear. He'd taken the time to shower and change, but not to sleep.

He walked into the office being used by Carl Briscoe and tossed an envelope on his desk.

The American looked up from what he was doing and tapped the envelope. "What's this?"

"A statement showing that I now have two hundred million dollars in an account at one of my banks."

He opened the envelope and studied the paper with a low whistle. "My compliments. I didn't think you could do it."

"I told you I could. Now what do we do?"

The American put the paper back on the desk. "Things are moving. I was just trying to call you when you walked in. I've made some contacts, and they tell me that both Juliana and the ambassador are still alive."

Alain's throat closed with emotion. "Did they tell you anything else?"

"They confirmed that she was shot and is apparently quite ill."

"Has she been seen by a doctor?"

"My contacts didn't know."

Alain paced back and forth, then stopped in front of the desk. "Who are these contacts?"

The American shook his head. "Look, I know you're worried. We all are. But I think the less you know, the better off you're going to be."

Alain took the paper and put it back into his pocket. "No. That's not how we're going to do this."

The other man lifted an eyebrow. "We're not? You have a better idea?"

"I don't know if it's better, but it's the way things are going to happen. I'm very much a part of this now and I want to know what's going on every step of the way. I also want it understood by both you and the kidnappers that they're not going to get a penny of this money until I know for a fact that both Juliana and the ambassador are all right."

The American leaned back in his chair. "As I've already told you, the bottom line for these people is money. What makes you think they care about the way you want to do things?''

"They want the money and I have it, but unless they can prove to my satisfaction that I'm going to get what I'm paying for, namely the Sheridans, they aren't going to get what they want. I think the knowledge that they're going to have to prove it to me at some point might also serve as a deterrent if they're planning on harming them."

"It might. But then again, it might not. These people are completely unpredictable. Frankly we don't ordinarily operate in the manner you're suggesting because of that very fact."

"In this instance, according to what you told me, you aren't supposed to be 'operating' at all."

"That's true. We're doing you and Mrs. Sheridan a favor by staying involved in this."

A corner of Alain's mouth lifted, but he wasn't amused. "As you say in America, let's cut to the chase. Spare me your protestations of goodwill. You're involved in this only because the taking of Ambassador Sheridan and Juliana is a big slap in the face for your country. I'm offering you a chance to get them back without it costing you anything and you accepted that offer. You agreed not because you give a damn about them, but because it's what's best for you and your world image. Now, if you don't mind, I'd like to stick to the business at hand."

"All right," the American said quietly. "But just let me say this. In a sense you're right, but in another sense you're wrong. I've known Ambassador Sheridan for twenty years. He was one of my professors in college. He was then and remains a person I admire and respect—and like. I don't want to see anything happen to him any more than you do."

Alain looked at him for a long time, as though trying to decide whether or not he could trust the American, then inclined his head. "I'm glad we understand each other. Now I want to know what the next step is."

The American sat up straight. "Well, the first thing I did after you left here the other day was contact that third party I told you about."

"What third party?"

"The Eastern Liberation Front."

"Why do you need a third party?"

"To help with the negotiations."

"I don't understand. Why go to them instead of directly to the people who have Juliana and her father?"

"Because our chance of getting them back unharmed is better. The ELF is trying to become a legitimate political force in the world. They want to put their reputation of terrorism behind them. For them to successfully negotiate the release of Ambassador Sheridan and his daughter would be an incredible political coup for them, both in their homeland and internationally."

"I see."

"The truth, pure and simple, however, is that there's no guarantee that you're going to walk away from this with any of your money."

"You already told me that. And I told you that the money isn't the issue for me. Their safe return is."

The American pursed his lips as he studied Alain. "You must love her very much," he said quietly.

Alain's expression remained unchanged. He rose without responding. "I'll expect to hear from you shortly."

"As soon as I know anything, you'll know it, too."

Juliana was sleeping when the door was opened and light glared in from the hallway beyond. Her father took her hand in his.

A man stood framed by the doorway.

He thrust his machine gun toward the open door then pointed it at them. His meaning was obvious. Juliana tried to get up, but fell back against the cot with a groan. The man hit her leg with his gun and screamed at her. The ambassador, knowing it would do no good to argue, picked his daughter up in his arms and carried her into the hall. The man prodded him in the back with his gun until they came to another room with concrete block walls, no windows and bare light bulbs suspended by cords from the ceiling. He closed the door as soon as they were in and sat in a chair near the door with his gun aimed at them, presumably to keep them from escaping.

The door opened and another man walked in carrying a cellular telephone with the receiver separated from the main pack. He plunked it onto a shoddily constructed wood table. "You," he said pointing at Juliana, "talk."

Her father, still holding her, carried her to a chair near the table and set her down. Every movement of her shoulder was like a knife twisting.

The telephone receiver was shoved in her direction.

Juliana raised it to her ear with a shaking hand. "Hello?" she said tentatively.

There was a long pause at the other end. So long that Juliana had already started to take the phone from her ear when she heard someone say her name. She quickly raised the phone. "Hello?" she said again.

"Juliana, are you all right?"

"Alain!" she said weakly. "What are you...I mean, how did you know that we were..." She couldn't seem to finish her sentence.

"Are you all right?" he asked more softly.

The gentleness in his voice was very nearly her undoing. "Yes," she said, choking back a sob.

"And your father? Have you seen him?"

"Yes. He's here with me now."

"Good. Have you seen a doctor?"

"No."

"All right. Listen carefully. A way is being worked out to bring you home. We don't know how long it's going to take, but it shouldn't be much longer. I—"

The man who'd brought in the phone abruptly snatched it from her.

"Alain," she cried out, tears filling her eyes.

"Juliana? Juliana?" Alain shouted into the phone. There was a click and the line went dead.

His hand tightened around the receiver.

"What is it?" the American asked.

He handed him the phone. "She's gone."

"How did she sound?"

"Not well. Her voice was weak." He stood there for several seconds, then slammed his fist on the desk. "If I ever get my hands on those bastards, so help me, I'll kill them for what they've done."

Carl was surprised into silence. Until now the Frenchman had been almost unnaturally calm. This was the first sign of emotion of any kind that he'd seen.

"I want her home now. She needs a doctor."

"I've already told you that we can't do that. This is going to take time."

"It's already taken too much time."

"It's going to take however long it's going to take."

Alain dragged his fingers through his hair. "I can't stand this waiting."

"I know." The American was sympathetic. "But we're playing by the kidnappers' rules right now, not our rules; their schedules, not ours."

Alain thought for a moment, then shook his head. "No."

"No what?"

"We're not playing by their schedule any longer. I want Juliana released. Call it a gesture of goodwill on their part."

"You can't be serious."

"I've never been more serious in my life. If she dies while in their custody, they aren't going to get any money."

"What about the ambassador?"

"He's their guarantee that they'll get the money even if they release Juliana."

"I don't know. I'll run it past the ELF and see if they can bring the kidnappers around."

"How long will that take?"

"I don't know."

"So we wait."

"We wait."

Alain walked to the window and stood staring outside.

Juliana's fever had disappeared for a time, but now it was back and worse than ever. Her father took the damp cloth from her forehead and dipped it into the basin of water the kidnappers had finally allowed. Rather than wringing the excess back into the basin, he held it over his daughter and let the water run over her face and throat. She raised her eyelids and smiled at him in the dim light of the battery-powered lantern that had been set near the cot. Or at least she tried to smile. She was so tired that even that took a lot of effort.

The door opened. A man stood there with a gun while another unarmed man entered. He went to Juliana and tried to lift her in his arms, but the ambassador grabbed him.

"Please," the man said in English. "I'm here to help you. Your daughter is being taken home."

He let go. "She needs a doctor desperately."

"I can see that. I'll make sure an ambulance is waiting for her." This time when the man tried to pick her up, the ambassador let him, and rose with her. He kissed her hot cheek. "You're going to be all right, Juliana," he whispered in her ear. "You're going to be safe."

She was too weak to protest being taken away from him. "What about you?"

He looked at the man holding her, who shook his head. "I'll probably be following you a little later on."

"Why can't we go together?"

"Because that's just the way it is." He looked at the man. "Please take care of her."

The man inclined his head and turned to leave. The door slammed shut after them. He heard the lock being turned and footsteps disappearing down the hall.

Juliana knew without opening her eyes that she was outside. She could feel the sun on her face and the cool breeze as it brushed against her skin. She wanted to ask where she was being taken, but couldn't seem to work up enough energy to get the words out.

She heard a car door being opened and then she was placed on a seat. She didn't even wince as her shoulder was bumped. She was, quite frankly, beyond pain.

And then the car was moving.

* * *

Alain was sitting in his office, unable to concentrate, Juliana's face kept flashing in front of his eyes. And that hair of hers. That beautiful, unruly hair.

As soon as his phone rang, he grabbed it.

"Alain, this is Carl. It's today."

"Finally. How's it being done?"

"She's being brought to a place in the country, just outside Paris. I've already called for an ambulance to meet them. They'll be by your office to pick you up any minute."

"I'm ready. Have you told Mrs. Sheridan yet?"

"No. I don't want to get her hopes up in case something goes wrong."

"I understand."

"Good luck."

Alain hung up. He sat absolutely still for a moment, then took a deep breath and left his office.

The car carrying Juliana stopped. The man who'd been driving got out. She heard voices, and then Alain was leaning into the car and looking down at her. He tried hard not to show his shock at her appearance, but didn't quite pull it off. In the short time she'd been gone, Juliana had lost perhaps fifteen pounds from her already slight frame. Her face was flushed and there were dark circles beneath her eyes. She had on the same clothes she'd worn the day she was taken, and they were caked in blood. One sleeve had been ripped off and her

wound clumsily bandaged. When she looked at him, her
eyes were glazed. She smiled and closed her eyes again.

Alain lifted her from the car and carried her in his
arms to the waiting ambulance. His mouth nuzzled her
hair. "You're going to be all right." He didn't know
who he was trying harder to convince—Juliana or himself.

The doctor who'd been waiting in the ambulance
went to work on her as soon as she was settled on the
stretcher in the back. As it bumped over the back roads
on its way to a main highway, he removed the bandage
and began cleaning the wound while a nurse set up an
IV and began pumping much-needed nutrients into her
body.

Alain tried to stay out of the way, but he wouldn't let
go of her hand. It was as though he could, by that contact, pour some of his own strength into her.

The trip seemed interminable to him. In fact it lasted
an hour. The minute they arrived at the hospital Juliana was whisked into surgery.

Alain went to a phone and dialed Juliana's mother.
"Brian," he said, recognizing his voice, "Juliana's been
returned. She's at the American Hospital in Neuilly.
Round up your family and get over here right away."

"She's going to be all right, isn't she?" Brian asked.

"I don't know." Alain cleared his throat. "She
looked very ill."

"Oh, God." It was obvious that Brian was trying to
hold himself together. "What about Dad?"

"He's still being held."

"Is he alive?"

"Yes. At least he was less than two hours ago, according to the man who brought Juliana to me."

"Thanks, Alain. I'll get Mom and bring her straight to the hospital."

Alain hung up the phone and went to the nurses' station. "Any word on the woman I just brought in?"

"She's only been in surgery for a few minutes," the nurse said kindly. "These things take time. I'm sure the doctor will come to you as soon as he's finished. Why don't you get yourself some coffee, or something to eat."

Alain didn't even respond. He just started pacing back and forth in the long hallway.

Less than half an hour later, Brian, his mother and the rest of the Sheridan family poured off of the elevator. Claire Sheridan went immediately to Alain and touched his arm. "How is she?"

Alain put his hand over hers. "I haven't heard anything since she was taken into surgery."

"Brian said that you told him she didn't look well."

"She didn't. I'm sorry."

Her eyes met and held his. She seemed to know without his saying anything exactly what was in his heart. "She's quite a fighter, you know. She always has been."

Alain nodded.

"She'll be fine. She has to be." Mrs. Sheridan managed a smile. "What would the world be like without Juliana?"

Alain turned away from her, not wanting her to see the sudden flash of pain he felt at the thought.

It was days before Juliana fully regained consciousness. She lay perfectly still as her awareness grew. She smelled the antiseptic. She heard quiet footsteps passing by beyond a closed door. She felt a hand holding hers.

Very slowly she opened her eyes. The hospital room was dimly lit. Turning her head just a little, she saw Alain sitting in a chair that had been pulled close to her bed. He had her hand cradled in both of his. His eyes stared hard at a wall with nothing on it.

Juliana moved her fingers and Alain's gaze flew to her face. His dark eyes warmed with pleasure and relief. "You're awake," he said softly as he lifted his other hand and touched her forehead.

She smiled at him.

"How do you feel?"

"Sleepy. Where am I?"

"In a hospital. You were brought here several days ago."

"You brought me, didn't you?"

"Yes."

"What about my father?"

"He's still being held, but as far as we know he's still safe. Arrangements are being made to bring him home."

"What arrangements?"

"Nothing you need to concern yourself with. He'll be home before you know it."

"You sound so sure."

"I am. These people want money. Once they have it, they'll have no reason to harm your father. In fact, if they do anything but release him, their credibility as kidnappers will be ruined."

"What an odd way of putting it."

"Who will pay them in the future if it's believed they'll simply kill their hostages regardless?"

"That makes sense." Her eyes met his. "Who are these people who took us?"

"They're called the Middle East Freedom Fighters."

"I've never heard of them."

"Neither had a lot of people until they snatched you and your father. Now they're on every news broadcast in the world."

Juliana shook her head. "I hope he's all right."

Alain touched her cheek. "Please, don't worry about your father. Everything that can be done is being done. You have to think about yourself right now, and getting better."

She sighed as her eyes rested on his darkly shadowed face. Lifting a hand, she ran it over the rough stubble. "You look terrible," she said with a smile.

He kissed the palm of her hand, then held it against his face. "I feel wonderful."

"When was the last time you went home to change your clothes?"

"What day is it?" he asked.

She smiled again. "So you were worried about me."

"Guilty."

"Good."

"Good?"

"It means you feel something for me after all."

He put her hand back onto the sheet. "I just want to see you happy and healthy again."

"That's all?"

"That's all."

Her mother looked in through the small window in the door and as soon as she saw that Juliana was conscious, she and every other Sheridan who was outside rushed into the room.

Alain rose and moved away from the bed. He watched for a few minutes, then quietly left.

Juliana saw him go. She started to call after him, but didn't. This was the way he wanted it and for now she had to just leave it alone.

Chapter Ten

Juliana stood staring out the window at the Paris street. It was late fall. The trees had nearly finished shedding their leaves and the wind, though innocent enough by Wisconsin standards, blew them every which way.

It had been nearly a month since she'd gotten out of the hospital, and three weeks since her father had been safely returned to his family. She was leaving for Wisconsin in the morning.

Her father came up behind her and put his hands on her shoulders, careful not to hurt her. "What are you thinking about as you stand here so quietly?" he asked.

She turned her head and smiled up at him. "Alain."

"Have you heard from him?"

"No. Not since I awoke in the hospital."

"Is that why you look so sad?"

She brushed her cheek against his hand. "I guess I was just hoping that he would have changed his mind about me. I was so sure that he was going to discover he was in love with me. Reality has lost a lot of its appeal lately."

"You give up too easily."

She shook her head. "I'm just tired of behaving like a moth that batters itself to death against a street lamp. The fact is that Alain doesn't want anything to do with me."

"He was there in the hospital."

"And he left as soon as I awoke."

Her father turned her around. "Juliana, I've found out some things recently and I've debated about telling you, but I think you have a right to know. It wasn't the government who came up with the money to secure our release."

"But I thought..."

"I know what you thought. I thought the same thing until that fellow from the State Department set me straight. It was Alain who paid the ransom."

Juliana just looked at him for a moment, at a loss for words. "The ransom was two hundred million dollars!"

"I know. He had to sell the château to raise it."

"Oh, no."

"And why do you think he'd do something like that? Out of friendship for me, or out of love for you?"

"I don't know. Why didn't he say anything?"

"You'll have to ask him that."

"He won't talk to me. I've called him at home and at the office and left messages but he never calls back."

"And you let that stop you?"

"Well, I . . ."

"The château hasn't changed hands yet, and I have it on good authority that he's there tonight."

"He'll never let me in."

"Then just walk in—and ask yourself why he's afraid to return your calls."

Juliana suddenly smiled and kissed her father on the cheek. "I think I'll ask him. Thank you."

"The driver's waiting for you."

There was a spring in her step as she walked away from him. She stopped in the doorway and turned around. "You once warned me away from Alain. What made you change your mind? The ransom he paid?"

"The sacrifice. How could I not want my only daughter to love a man who would give up everything for her?"

In thoughtful silence, Juliana went out to the car. The chauffeur opened the rear door for her then climbed into the front seat next to the armed guard her father sent everywhere with her. She didn't have to say anything. The driver knew exactly where he was going.

Juliana leaned back in her seat and stared out the window at Paris. It was night. The street lamps were lit. It amazed her how the city had managed to remain so charming and pretty. Certainly there were occasional lapses where towering buildings scarred it, but for the most part it remained the Paris of the centuries.

City quickly turned to countryside. As they drew closer to the château, Juliana began to get nervous. She was sure she was doing the right thing, but that didn't necessarily make it any easier. She felt a little like she was going there to say, "here I am, Alain. Reject me yet again." Frankly she didn't know if she could go through that again.

But she knew she would if she had to.

When the car stopped in front of the château, the driver opened the door for her. Juliana stepped onto the gravel and stood there gathering her courage. Straightening her shoulders—and wincing at the discomfort in the one that had been injured—she took a deep breath and headed for the front door. "You can leave," she said over her shoulder. "I won't be needing you anymore tonight."

Marcel opened the door and looked at her in pleased surprise. "Miss Juliana, what are you doing here?"

"Hello, Marcel. I'd like to see Alain."

"Oh, dear, I don't think so."

"I know he's here."

"Yes, but he doesn't want to be disturbed by anyone."

"Please." Her lovely eyes pleaded with him. "I'm leaving the country tomorrow. I have to talk to him before I go."

Marcel's wife appeared in the foyer behind him. As soon as she saw Juliana, she pushed past her husband to wrap Juliana in her great arms. "How are you?" she finally managed in English as she pulled Juliana into the house, ignoring her husband completely.

"I'm almost healed. Thank you for the wonderful cakes you sent. I put on nearly all the weight I'd lost."

Genvieve stood back, still holding Juliana's hands in hers, and gave her the once-over, shaking her head and clicking her tongue. "You are still too skinny. I'll bake some more."

Juliana smiled warmly at her. "You're so kind. I'm afraid I won't be here to eat them, though."

"Why not?"

"I was just telling your husband that I'm leaving for Wisconsin in the morning."

"Non!"

"Yes. It's time I got back to my own home. I've been away far too long. I'd like to see the Duc before I go."

"Of course you would," she said with a nod as she turned to look at her husband. "Tell her where he is."

Marcel said something in French.

Genvieve cut him off in midsentence, throwing her words at him in a way only the French can do when they're angry.

When she finished, Marcel raised his eyes to the ceiling and shook his head, then looked at Juliana. "I'll take you to him. If I don't, my wife will have me eating fast food."

Genvieve crossed her arms over her ample chest. "And don't you forget it," she said with a wink at Juliana.

Gearing herself up once again, Juliana followed Marcel up the stairs and down the long hall. He stopped in front of a door and turned to her. "Are you ready?" he asked.

She nodded.

"Good luck," he said quietly, and then knocked.

"Yes?"

"There's someone here to see you, sir."

"Who is it?"

"Miss Sheridan."

"Tell her I'm not in."

Juliana stepped past the butler and opened the door. "It's too late," she said quietly. "You know how pushy we Americans are."

Alain was standing near the window in a bedroom that was dark except for the light from the fireplace.

"Juliana, I ... How are you?"

"Much better since the last time you saw me, thank you. I don't need a sling anymore."

"You're looking well."

Marcel closed the door quietly behind her as Juliana crossed the room to where Alain was standing. "I had an interesting conversation with my father this evening."

Alain was silent, his eyes on hers.

"He told me that you raised the money to free us. He told me that you had to sell your home."

Alain shook his head. "I did, but I've gotten it back again. The Eastern Liberation Front managed to coax the MEFF into returning most of the money. They kept only a few million.''

''That's hardly the point. Why did you do it in the first place?''

Alain walked away from her to stand in front of the fireplace. ''I can't answer that.''

''Can't or won't?''

''Can't *and* won't.''

Juliana followed him. ''Alain, why is it so hard for you to admit to yourself that you love me?''

He shook his head.

She stood in front of him. ''You do, you know.''

His dark eyes burned through her. ''Juliana, just leave it alone and get out of here.''

''I'm not going.''

''Yes, you are.'' He grabbed her upper arm with the intention of turning her around to face the door. Juliana gasped in pain and Alain's hands immediately fell to his sides. ''Oh, Juliana, I'm sorry. I didn't mean to hurt you.''

She looked into his eyes and shook her head. ''Then why do you keep doing it again and again? Why do you keep turning away from me? I need to know. Is it Noelle?''

''Noelle?'' he asked blankly, then shook his head. ''I haven't seen Noelle since before you left France the last time. I haven't seen any woman.'' Alain cupped her face in his hand and moved his eyes over her face feature by feature, as though committing the whole to memory.

Juliana moved closer to him and put her hands on his chest.

He rubbed his thumb over her softly parted lips as his own drew closer. She was so near he could feel her sweet breath. "Oh, Juliana," he said softly as his mouth finally captured hers.

Her body melted against his and her arms went around his neck as his fingers tangled in her soft hair, drawing her more deeply into the kiss. Her lips left his to rain kisses down his throat and chest, unbuttoning his shirt as she went. He groaned and pulled her back up to his mouth, tasting her; exploring every corner and letting her do the same. She moved against him, feeling his need and wanting more.

Alain inhaled sharply and lifted her in his arms. His mouth never leaving hers, he carried her to the bed to lay her gently on it. With his head on the pillow beside hers, he ran his fingers through her hair as he gazed into her eyes. Neither of them spoke, but what Juliana saw in his eyes was enough. It filled her with joy. He gently kissed the corner of her mouth, then looked into her eyes again before capturing her lips completely.

Their bodies twined together, straining passionately against each other. Alain's mouth left hers to move along the line of her jaw to her ear. She felt his warm breath and his tongue, and then he moved lower, unbuttoning her blouse. His mouth followed the soft swell of her breast as his hand moved down her back and over her hips. Lifting her full skirt, he moved his hand along the length of her thigh to the soft skin between her legs.

Juliana inhaled sharply against his lips.

That sound seemed to reach somewhere deep inside Alain. He raised his head and looked down at her. With exquisite gentleness, he lowered her skirt and just held her quietly in his arms.

Juliana's body ached with unfulfilled desire for this man who was so near, and yet suddenly so far away from her.

She started to say something, but he just held her closer and whispered "sssshhh" against her ear as his hand stroked her hair.

After a while, the ache eased. She was able to relax her body against his. Moving her head away from his shoulder, she looked into his eyes.

Alain kissed her on the forehead and rose from the bed. "Come on. I'll take you home."

"Take me home? Why?"

"Because this isn't right."

"Isn't right?" she asked softly. "Nothing has ever been more right."

"Please, Juliana, don't argue with me. Not now. I want you to go home."

Without saying anything else, Juliana got to her feet. There were no words to describe what she was feeling. At that moment, she wanted desperately to be alone.

Alain took her hand in his and led her from the room and outside to his car. In silence he drove her to Paris and walked her to the door of her parents' home.

Juliana turned to him just before going inside. "I guess this is goodbye. My plane leaves tomorrow morning at ten."

"I hope you have a safe flight."

She started to say something, but the words wouldn't come. She looked into his eyes and then, shaking her head, she went inside and closed the door between them. Leaning her back against it, she stood there for a long time, beyond tears.

Alain went to his car and started the engine. But he didn't go anywhere. He just sat there with his hands gripping the steering wheel. What was happening to him?

Morning couldn't come soon enough for Juliana. She wanted to get out of France with something approaching desperation. By the time she came downstairs, she had her suitcases with her.

Her father took the one she was carrying in her left hand as soon as he saw her. "You have no business lifting something like this yet," he scolded.

"I'm fine."

He looked at her pale face. It told him everything he needed to know. "Oh, honey," he said, "I'm so sorry."

"I don't want to talk about it."

"It might make you feel better."

She kissed his cheek. "No, it won't. I need to sort this out alone."

"All right. I'll get my coat and your mother and I will take you to the airport."

Juliana caught his arm as he started to walk away. "No, Dad, please. I'd rather go alone."

"Are you sure?"

She nodded.

Her father understood her so well. "All right. Just let me get your mom."

Juliana took her own lightweight coat from the closet in the hallway and had just finished putting it on when both of her parents came into the foyer. Her mother hugged and kissed her. "I'm going to miss you."

"I'll miss you, too, Mom."

"Promise me that you'll take care of yourself."

"I will." She managed a reassuring smile.

Her father hugged her as well. "If you change your mind about talking, I'm as close as the nearest phone."

"I know. I'll call soon."

They walked her out to the car. The last image Juliana carried with her was of her parents standing on the steps with their arms around each other waving good-bye.

When they got to the airport, her father's driver carried her luggage into the terminal for her, then left. Juliana checked the bags through to Milwaukee then headed for her gate, completely preoccupied, oblivious to the people around her.

Alain ran into the airport a few minutes later and went to the ticket counter. "I need to know which airline has a flight leaving for the United States at ten o'clock."

The woman turned to the man at the window next to her and asked him. He checked the monitor in front of him. To Alain, it seemed to take forever.

"Air France has one leaving from Gate 44C. It's about ready to begin boarding."

"Thank you." Racing through the terminal, he dodged luggage and travelers, his eyes searching for Juliana. He rushed past people on the escalator as he climbed the moving stairs two at a time, then raced down the next terminal.

He spotted Juliana way ahead of him and shouted her name, but it was impossible to make himself heard above the noise of the other travelers. He ran faster, swearing softly when he was brought to a standstill by a crowd of people whose bodies formed a wall.

Juliana placed her purse and carry-on bag on the X-ray conveyor and walked through the metal detector. A woman at the other end smiled and handed Juliana her things, then she continued toward her gate with a quicker pace when she heard her flight being announced for boarding.

She thought she heard someone shout her name and turned to look, but didn't see anyone there.

Alain finally lost his patience and shoved someone aside so he could get through, apologizing as he did it. He ran through the metal detector and it went off. The guard made him come back and empty his pockets, which he did, tossing his keys and money into a small tray, then going through the metal detector again. "I'll come back for that," he called over his shoulder as he raced down the concourse without getting his keys or money.

Juliana handed the man at the gate her boarding pass and showed her passport. He let her through and she started down the long walk to the plane.

Alain called her name again and tried to run past the gate agent, but his path was blocked.

He could see her. "Juliana!" he yelled.

She turned and saw Alain struggling to get to her.

"Don't go," he yelled.

At first she couldn't believe what she was hearing.

He stopped struggling and just looked at her. "Please, don't go. I love you."

Juliana walked toward him, slowly at first, then broke into a run. She dropped her things to the ground and ran into his outstretched arms. Alain held her tightly against him. "I love you," he said again. Looking into her joyful face, he laughed and kissed the tip of her nose. "Come with me. We need to talk."

No one understood love like the French. The gate agent had retrieved her things and handed them to Alain. He collected his money and keys from the security guard and, with his arm around Juliana's waist, walked her out of the building and settled her into his illegally parked car.

Juliana remained silent as Alain maneuvered them away from the airport. Every once in a while, he'd look at her and they'd smile at each other, but nothing was said.

He took her back to the Château de Lumiere, but instead of driving to the house, he drove across the grounds to the edge of the forest, then stopped the car and helped Juliana out. With her hand in his, he walked her along the path to the stream, settling her onto the grass beside it.

Alain didn't sit, but stood staring into the water for a long time before finally turning to Juliana. "I wanted to bring you here to tell you what's in my heart because this is where I first saw you. And this is where I fell in love with you." He hunkered down in front of her and cupped her chin in his hand. "You are so beautiful," he said softly. "You have this inner light that radiates all around you." He let go of her chin and stood again. "You know, all of my life I've avoided getting close to anyone. When I was young, of course, I craved closeness with my family, but they just weren't capable of it. Over the years, the people closest to me were the ones my parents paid to take care of me. I kept myself distant from them because I was always aware that if my parents stopped paying them, they'd leave. I cut myself off from other people, at first because I was afraid to feel anything for them, and later because I was incapable of feeling anything for them. At least I thought I was until you showed up."

He knelt in front of her again. "You turned my world upside down from the first moment I saw you. I felt the same pull you did, but didn't know how to deal with it. It was easier for me to deny its existence."

"You nearly broke my heart."

"I'm so sorry," he said softly. "I thought if I pushed you far enough away, the feelings would go away, too. But they didn't. They grew stronger every time I saw you. And I got angry with you for causing me to feel things I didn't want to feel. I was actually relieved when you went back to Wisconsin. I figured I was safe."

"And then I came back."

His dark eyes warmed her. "And then you came back, and it started all over again. When you walked into that room with your father..." He searched for the words. "When I saw you again, it was as though I'd been dead inside without realizing it, and you brought me back to life. It made me resent you all the more. It meant that I didn't have control any longer. Someone else had the control. You."

"You looked at me as though you hated me."

"I did. And I thought that if I could just stay away from you until you left France, my life would return to normal. And it almost did for a time—until I found out about your abduction." He shook his head. "Juliana, I didn't know if you were alive or dead. What I did discover in that moment was how very much you meant to me. It didn't matter whether or not I wanted you in my heart. You were already there. Getting you home safely was the only thing that mattered to me. Nothing was too high a price to pay for that."

"But when I came back, you turned away from me again. Why?"

"I saw you with your family. There's such closeness among all of you. My background is so different. I just thought you'd be better off with someone more like your family. Someone who can let himself feel without qualification.''

"So you left.'' She looked into his eyes. "Why did you send me away last night?''

"Because you scared the hell out of me.'' Alain pushed her hair away from her forehead. "I wanted you so badly last night that I still burn inside. But I knew, even then, that if we did make love, there would be no turning back for me. And I still didn't think that I was what was best for you.''

"And yet you came after me today.''

"I was up all night. I couldn't get you out of my thoughts. I tried to imagine what my life was going to be like without you in it, and there was nothing but emptiness.'' He looked into her eyes. "Juliana Sheridan, the simple truth is that I love you. You've aroused emotions in me that I never thought myself capable of. I want us to have a houseful of children. I want to get closer to you than ever a man and woman have gotten before. I don't want to know where I end and you begin.'' He shook his head and rubbed his thumb against her damp cheek. "See what you've done to me?''

Juliana rose onto her knees and felt his arms close around her as she buried her face in his neck. "I love you so much.''

"Then say you'll marry me.''

"I'll marry you.''

Alain held her away from him. A smile curved his mouth as he looked at her. "Oh, Juliana, who would ever have thought when I, in all innocence, offered your father the use of my home, that I was destined to fall in love with the ambassador's daughter?''

"Kiss me."

"I think I'd better marry you first."

"Coward."

"Be warned," he said softly, "you're playing with fire."

Her lips moved closer to his. "I know."

"Juliana..."

She came closer. Her lips were only inches from his. "Now say no," she dared him.

It took him several seconds, but he finally managed it. "No," he said as he straightened away from her and got to his feet, pulling Juliana up with him. "We're not going to start something we can't finish. Doing that once was hard enough."

Juliana rested the palm of her hand against his cheek. She didn't need to say anything. It was in her eyes for him to read.

Alain covered her hand with his and looked into her eyes. What Juliana saw there filled her with a happiness like none she'd ever known before. This was the way it was supposed to be. The way she'd known it had to be from the first moment she'd seen him.

Epilogue

Juliana stood in the garden watching her husband and their twin son and daughter playing a rousing game of tag. Alain fell exhausted onto the grass and laughed while the children climbed all over him. Slowly they grew more still, then the children, one on either side of their father, fell asleep.

Alain lay there with them for a time, then rose and lifted one in each arm. He smiled when he saw his wife watching.

"They missed their naps," he said quietly.

"I know."

They went into the house together, and into the wing they'd transformed into a real home, right down to the overstuffed furniture. The children's room was next to their own room. Alain put Sophia into one crib and Edouard into another, then stood back and gazed down at them while Juliana pulled their blankets up and ran her hands gently over their tiny backs.

She moved next to Alain and touched his hand. He looked at her and pulled her into his arms.

"What are you thinking?" she asked quietly.

"It's hard to explain."

"Try."

Alain smiled at his wife. "I always do for you. I was watching our children, and thinking how much I love them and how much I like being their father." His fingers gently traced her face. "And how much I love being married to their mother." He shook his head. "It seems the more I love, the more I'm able to love."

"It happens that way."

"Every morning when I wake with you in my arms is like a miracle to me. And when I see these amazing children that we created out of the love we feel for each other it's yet another miracle."

"Why, Alain de Bournier, you sound almost romantic."

"And it's all your fault." His mouth closed over hers in a lingering kiss. "How is it that the more I make love to you, the more I want to make love to you?"

Juliana tangled her fingers in his thick hair. "We have some time before the children wake," she whispered against his mouth.

"I love you so much." His voice was thick with emotion. "Thank you for coming into my life."

She touched his face. "Now do you believe in destiny?"

"Enough to know that you're mine." He lifted her in his arms. "And do you know what your destiny is going to be for at least the next hour?"

"I hope so," she said with a smile.

"Oh," he said shaking his head, "you're certainly not the shy young woman I married."

"Thank you."

"Your smile has even grown saucier."

"It's all that anticipation."

"Well, let's put an end to that right now."

"I'm with you."

"Now and forever."

* * * * *

COMING NEXT MONTH

#706 NEVER ON SUNDAE—Rita Rainville
A Diamond Jubilee Title!
Heather Brandon wanted to help women lose weight. But lean, hard
Wade Mackenzie had different ideas. He wanted Heather to lose her
heart—to him!

#707 DOMESTIC BLISS—Karen Leabo
By working as a maid, champion of women's rights Spencer Guthrie
tried to prove he practiced what he preached. But could he convince
tradition-minded Bonnie Chapman that he loved a woman like her?

#708 THE MARK OF ZORRO—Samantha Grey
Once conservative Sarah Wingate saw "the man in the mask" she
couldn't keep her thoughts on co-worker Jeff Baxter. But then she
learned he and Zorro were one and the same!

#709 A CHILD CALLED MATTHEW—Sara Grant
Laura Bryant was determined to find her long-lost son at any cost.
Then she discovered the key to the mystery lay with Gareth Ryder, the
man who had once broken her heart.

#710 TIGER BY THE TAIL—Pat Tracy
Sarah Burke had grown up among tyrants, so Lucas Rockworth's
gentle demeanor drew her like a magnet. Soon, however, she learned
her lamb roared like a lion!

#711 SEALED WITH A KISS—Joan Smith
Impetuous Jodie James was off with stuffy—but handsome!—Greg
Edison to look for their missing brothers. Jodie knew they were a
mismatched couple, but she was starting to believe the old adage that
opposites attract....

AVAILABLE THIS MONTH:

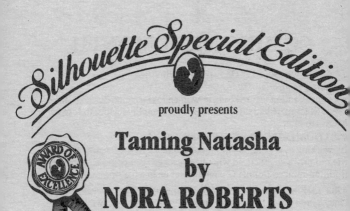

Silhouette Special Edition

proudly presents

Taming Natasha
by
NORA ROBERTS

In March, award-winning author Nora Roberts weaves her special brand of magic in TAMING NATASHA (SSE #583). Natasha Stanislaski was a pussycat with Spence Kimball's little girl, but to Spence himself she was as ornery as a caged tiger. Would some cautious loving sheath her claws and free her heart from captivity?

TAMING NATASHA, by Nora Roberts, has been selected to receive a special laurel—the Award of Excellence. Look for the distinctive emblem on the cover. It lets you know there's something truly special inside.

Available in March at your favorite retail outlet, or order your copy by sending your name, address, zip or postal code, along with a check or money order for $2.95, plus 75¢ postage and handling, payable to Silhouette Reader Service to:

In the U.S.
901 Fuhrmann Blvd.
Box 1396
Buffalo, NY 14269-1396

In Canada
P.O. Box 609
Fort Erie, Ontario
L2A 5X3

Please specify book title with your order.

TAME-1

DIAMOND JUBILEE
CELEBRATION!

It's Silhouette Books' tenth anniversary, and what better way to celebrate than to toast *you*, our readers, for making it all possible. Each month in 1990, we'll present you with a DIAMOND JUBILEE Silhouette Romance written by an all-time favorite author!

Welcome the new year with *Ethan*—a LONG, TALL TEXANS book by Diana Palmer. February brings Brittany Young's *The Ambassador's Daughter*. Look for *Never on Sundae* by Rita Rainville in March, and in April you'll find *Harvey's Missing* by Peggy Webb. Victoria Glenn, Lucy Gordon, Annette Broadrick, Dixie Browning and many more have special gifts of love waiting for you with their DIAMOND JUBILEE Romances.

Be sure to look for the distinctive DIAMOND JUBILEE emblem, and share in Silhouette's celebration. Saying thanks has never been so romantic....

SRJUB-1

SILHOUETTE DESIRE

Another bride for a Branigan brother!

"Why did you stop at three Branigan books?"
S. Newcomb from Fishkill, New York, asks.

We didn't! We brought you Jody's story, Desire #523,
BRANIGAN'S TOUCH in October 1989.

"Did Leslie Davis Guccione write any more books
about those Irish Branigan brothers?"
B. Willford from Gladwin, Michigan, wants to know.

And the answer is yes! In March you'll get a chance to
read Matt's story, Desire #553—

PRIVATE PRACTICE
by Leslie Davis Guccione

**You won't want to miss it because
he's the last Branigan brother!**

BRAN-1

м

At long last, the books you've been waiting for by one of America's top romance authors!

DIANA PALMER
DUETS

Ten years ago Diana Palmer published her very first romances. Powerful and dramatic, these gripping tales of love are everything you have come to expect from Diana Palmer.

In March, some of these titles will be available again in DIANA PALMER DUETS—a special three-book collection. Each book will have two wonderful stories plus an introduction by the author. You won't want to miss them!

 Silhouette Books®

DP-1